One for Rose Cottage

By

Shelby Locke

An environmentally friendly book printed and bound in England by
www.printondemand-worldwide.com

Mixed Sources
Product group from well-managed forests, and other controlled sources
www.fsc.org Cert no. TT-COC-002641
© 1996 Forest Stewardship Council

PEFC Certified
This product is from sustainably managed forests and controlled sources
www.pefc.org

This book is made entirely of chain-of-custody materials

www.fast-print.net/store.php

One for Rose Cottage

ISBN 978-178035-623-5

E mail: shelbylocke@sky.com
www.shelbylocke.co.uk
www.oneforrosecottage.com

Second edition. 2013

First published 2013 by
FASTPRINT PUBLISHING
Peterborough, England.

Contents:

'Cry for the little girl who lived in the ground
Cry for the little girl who has now been found
Cry for the little girl who lives all alone
Cry for the little girl who was trapped by the stone
Cry for the little girl who lost all her kin
Cry for the little girl who hides from her sin'

'The only true way to return after death,
is in the memory of others'

Our time on Earth is but a blink
Sometimes not enough to think
And through those left upon their wake
Memories of their lives we make
So think often of those gone by
Never let their memories die!

Julie Ann Peckham
3/5/1963 – 21/11/2012

Acknowledgements

With special thanks to the following:

Jez, forever grateful for your help… past and future!

Suzy Shuttleworth, for her invaluable input and advice about One for Rose Cottage!

Steve Earley for his tireless help and support.

Stephen & Susan Keyes of the Silver Plough, Pitton.

Martyn Dean of 'Jack's Bush Forge'

Nina Thomas of Rose Cottage, Saundersfoot, Pembrokeshire

As always, to the following for their involvement: Marina Summers, Graham & Vivienne Hockley and Shirley Pike.

A special mention to Tanya Pike of Misty Design for her creative flare and the resulting book cover!

To Ady, Jo and Caleb… forever in my heart!

Hey Marnie Smith…! You're next!

One For Rose Cottage

Following personal heartbreak in the horror that was 9/11, Rose Cottage and Claire Chambers become inextricably linked. Rose Cottage holds a secret and Claire Chambers is the only person who can reveal the mystery that surrounds it. She has been chosen to 'open a door', which some would rather leave closed and are prepared to do almost anything to keep it that way.

Claire now walks a path others have trodden, but have not survived unscathed. The path is littered with broken hearts, dreams and lives… For some, there cannot be peace until the final mystery is solved and Claire must find a way to do this without being drawn into a situation where the path has no way back.

All is not as it seems at Rose Cottage, and nor will it be until the bitter and bloody end.

Chapter 1

Life Changing Experiences

My story does not really start until the day I bought Rose Cottage, a thatched lodge of beauty, wonderment and mystery.

Leading up to and until then, there were many changes in my life.

In such a short period of time, my life changed from me being a carefree, adventurous girl, to a woman with untold responsibilities. These transformations were memorable to say the least. The fact is, none of these changes were expected.

Before I get to that, I must explain a little bit more about myself and how I eventually succeeded in purchasing my dream house, which was to turn out to be the start of the adventure of my lifetime.

My name is Claire Chambers, aka Kookie. Much like my Mother, I am tall and slim, but have my Father's dark hair and green eyes. My nickname had an association with the work I did back then. However, in truth, I originally earned my nickname from my Father who, so he said, was a fan of a TV show from the late 1950s to the mid 1960s. Apparently, *77 Sunset Strip*, was a 'must see' on cable when Mum and Dad visited America on their many business trips. Mum hated the name, but Dad and I knew this as our special pet name for me. I loved hearing him call out, "Kookie, where are you?" Sometimes he would say, "Kookie, Daddy's home!" These familiar calls often meant I had a present awaiting me as I rushed to greet him on the doorstep. Anyhow, in those days my pseudonym was spelt with a K…, you know, Kookie. It had something to do with the fact that I loved brushing my hair when I was younger, just like my American on-screen namesake. By all accounts, the young rookie spent a lot of time combing his hair in between helping solve crimes! Still, my friends who, like me, knew little of its origin later adapted this, and I was eventually 're-invented' as Cookie with a C. As I grew up, I somehow felt more associated to the latter since it then mirrored my life and work with computers. Sadly, though, my nickname was lost to all since it came to reflect a tragedy in my life and from then on, I expressly banned it. Computers have always been part of my life, and their influence has kept me on a route I can only describe as awesome. By the age of sixteen, I was prepared to bypass college and jump straight into a career. This I did, and after a short recruitment process, Remote Universal Security Systems Elite Ltd, R.U.S.S.E.L for short, employed me. There were few objections from my parents since they spent much of their time abroad. That is not to say that they didn't care, because I know they did. They just knew that I was a free spirit with a whole life ahead of me. Dad's only advice to me was, "Look after number one. Oh, and don't get caught." I remember the peals of laughter after he said that.

Within days of starting work, I realised what a self-defeating, mind-numbing chore the workplace was. I soon found myself forever having to appease a bunch of self-serving, ass-kissing load of backbiters. Don't get me wrong, I loved my work, just not my colleagues. Mostly they all complied with a certain criteria, as laid down by faceless morons who know nothing about anything in particular, but know how to exploit people to their own advantage. I am convinced the only reason these types are where they are today is because, they either had one good idea for a business, a friend in the know, or had money to start with. As for the rest of us, we all did our best to make them money in the hopes that they kept employing us to make them more money. This vicious cycle was one I would eventually break free from… but for very unexpected reasons.

The company I worked for specialised in, of all things, computer security. My boss wrote the original software, which allowed other businesses to manage all incoming and outgoing computer traffic and security. This, somehow, makes what I have to say even more incredible since my own personal computer was, at all times, safeguarded to the hilt with anti-viral software. I made sure I would never fall victim to some type of scam or security breach, so I insisted that I had the very best software of its type.

For me though, it is all about the freedom the computer gives me. In my world, I own the system, which means I am in total control of what goes on around me. Generally, the technology has allowed me the autonomy to explore a world I know so little about. Seeing and reading about other cultures and ways of life has, over the years, opened my eyes to the many things I had no idea existed. From my home or office, I could escape my day-to-day, humdrum life for something better and see things I could only dream of. Personally, I loved my computer as one would love a best friend. This, perversely, gave me the right to dominate and order it to do what I want, when I wanted to. As I have already mentioned, it also took me places I had never a hope of ever going. I could, if I so wished, explore the depths of space or the intricacies of the human body. I even developed another form of life, by means of a graphical representation. She was an Avatar, only known to a few. *Finitia* was fashioned from the deepest recesses of my mind, and I gave her special powers I only wished I had. Sadly, as time went by, she became a victim of growing up and life in general.

Anyhow, as I had already indicated there was soon to be sadness in my life. This was a sadness I could not nullify by Avatars, a good movie or copious amounts of chocolate. One year after I started work and two weeks after my seventeenth birthday, unfolding events would change my life forever.

My week, like many others, started well and meeting up with Joel, my good and wonderful friend from childhood, was cathartic as he had loads to tell me about his weekend. Joel D'Arcy was the second greatest influence in my life, but for now, I shall concentrate on what followed.

It was a few days after meeting up with Joel that the news, which would have the greatest impact on my life, reached me. 11th of September 2001 started as uneventful as I would expect for a Tuesday. My parents were away on one of their many overseas trips. When I first heard the news of the unfolding disaster in New York, it shocked me, like everyone around me, to the core. What made this event so shocking was that my parents were, on that day, in New York. But even more shattering, and unbeknownst to me at the time, was that they were both in the World Trade Centre during the devastating terrorist attacks.

And although that knowledge of their exact whereabouts was unknown to me, I somehow felt that something was wrong and ran home from work. On my return home, I found Nanny Rose waiting impatiently by the phone. She was clearly agitated. Normally, I would stay at her house while my parents were away, but on this occasion, she was staying at my parents instead. It's strange the things you remember, but I do recall she had a problem with her boiler.

Nanny Rose said she'd had a phone call from Mum to say that she was in the South Tower of the World Trade Centre! Mum said she was worried, as she couldn't reach Dad who had been conducting a separate business transaction in the North Tower. She explained that from where she was standing, she could see fire spreading upwards in the North Tower. Not long after that the line went dead and no matter how many times Nan tried, she couldn't get her back on the phone. Nan even used the internet to see if she could find the telephone number of the business Mum had been visiting, but to no avail. As it turned out, contact via the landline would have been just as impossible as calling Mum on her mobile. I didn't know what to say - her calm exterior belied the fear for her son, and my Mother - I knew that she must be terrified.

Nan's ability to use the internet was a result of her trying to understand my love of computers. A few years back she was so curious about it that I decided to teach her the basics, although once she grasped that she was away.

We sat in horror, side-by-side in front of the television, as news slowly filtered through. We tried not to fear the worst yet somehow knew there was more to come. This event had a devastating effect on thousands like us, but I suppose at the time we didn't see it that way, as we simply concentrated our thoughts on the only two people we knew who were involved. Later, and more shockingly, I would learn that they never found Dad's body. Mum, on the other hand, survived long enough for Nanny Rose to get me to New York to see her before she died.

The mere fact that we made it to that hospital, was purely down to the sheer bloody mindedness of Nanny Rose. You see, we could sit no longer and watch the tragedy unfurl. As a result, we instinctively rushed to the airport, knowing Mum and Dad were in trouble and needed us. En route, we were fortunate enough to hear from a business friend of my Father, who told us the name of the hospital where Mum had been admitted. I vividly remember Nan frantically scribbling down as many details as she could, which would subsequently help us on our arrival. How they knew how to contact us was a mystery I wouldn't solve until much later.

When we finally got to London's Heathrow Airport, there were many reasons to doubt our sanity since we didn't have the full facts to hand, we just knew we had to get to New York. The airlines had acted almost immediately and brought in stringent security measures to counteract a possible global attack from the air. I feared that we would never reach Mum and listened intently every time an announcement came over the intercom. Couple this with a constant frenzy of activity, and that fact that Heathrow had grounded all aircraft heading to America. I became frantic. This latest news indicated that our efforts had been futile and therefore our presence at the airport was pointless. Well, I thought that was the case, until Nanny Rose then made another decision and demanded tickets for the next available flight to Canada. We made the last flight outward bound since, by now, even domestic flights were being cancelled as an emergency reaction to the attacks. It was as if Nanny Rose had weaved magic. Magic which granted us the power to get there.

Our flight was smooth, but there was an understandable amount of nervousness and tension as people eyed each other with distrust. Passengers were restricted from getting up from their seats, except for essential needs. And as more information reached the authorities, we were further restricted; passengers found themselves being closely monitored and escorted to and from the toilets by an attendant, which only increased the tension onboard. Even then, they were only allowed to do so after complying with an order to ring for attention and wait for assistance when a comfort break was required. And on a long-haul flight like this, tension seemed to reach breaking point.

As we approached North American airspace, we noticed two F-15s, each flying either side of our aircraft. They stayed with us until we approached the main runway in Toronto before they disappeared from sight. I will never forget the sight of them. As the flight touched down there was a loud cheer from the majority of the passengers. I, for one, failed to see anything to cheer about, although I fully understood their relief at landing safely.

We hired a car to make the trip from Toronto to the US border, and then to New York. It was mostly uneventful until we reached immigration. Here, an officer routinely questioned us about our intentions and were only allowed through when Nanny Rose had a quiet word with the chief officer. As they spoke, he glanced my way before scanning through our passports again. Eventually, he signalled for a colleague to take us into another room and asked us to wait. Here, our passports were finally stamped and a friendly, if concerned, smile sent us on our way.

Only four hundred and eighty miles stood between us and our final destination. These miles couldn't pass quickly enough for me, I was agitated. Nanny Rose showed no such agitation, at least outwardly. I am certain the only reason she remained so calm was for my sake. In some ways, I wished she had dropped the façade and told me what she was really thinking, so that we could both disclose our true feelings. On reflection, I suppose without Nan's strength of character, we wouldn't have been where we were at that point. So, for that, I was and shall be eternally grateful.

Eventually, exhausted we reached New York, and following the scribbled instructions made our way through the hectic roads to the hospital. Many times we found that roads were cordoned off, that terrible grey dust covered everything, and I struggled to control my panic. When we finally arrived, I forced myself to stay calm. There are only two words to describe what greeted us when we reached the hospital… chaos, and horror. The silence of the many patients on beds and stretchers dotted around was terrible, the place was crowded with the walking wounded. Nurses and doctors were doing their best to treat the injured and control the situation. Every face around showed signs of shock and total disbelief.

A glassy-eyed, wild-haired woman came over to me and asked, "Have you seen my Joseph? He was standing next to me earlier." I, of course, shook my head and she immediately left my side to approach another before asking the same question. The day-old, dusty debris on her cheeks was streaked with a combination of blood, tears and mascara, which had then congealed into a thick dark crust by her chin. Bizarrely this gave her the look of a badly made-up clown and I felt a mixture of complete horror and total sadness.

The sight of the woman had scared me and her appearance caused me to conjure up all sorts of horrible images in my head. Given these thoughts, I feared what would greet us when we finally saw Mum. We still hadn't heard anything about my Dad. We waited and waited, and it felt like forever. I held Nan's hand, but her composure never once faltered. Finally we were called and led to a ward. It was then that I started to shake - I was so frightened at what we would see. Mum lay still, and if it hadn't have been for the grey dust in her auburn hair and covering her face, and the sounds of the machines that were keeping her alive, it would have appeared that she was sleeping. My initial relief turned to devastation though, when a nurse quietly explained the extent of her injuries. She said we should prepare ourselves.

I seem to remember specific moments about Mum's death, although the noises coming from the machines designed to monitor her vital levels seem so loud in my mind when I think back. I vividly remember Mum opening her pale blue eyes for a brief second before she took her last breath. She seemed to search the room, trying hard to focus, before seeing us. My heart jumped! She knew we were here! She would be okay! And then a passing battle-hardened nurse said, 'Hey, that happens sometimes…' She also said something about us being grateful for her not knowing anything. I don't think she meant to sound insensitive, she had already seen so much tragedy, but I remember wanting to scream at her. The last bit of hope I'd felt had been snatched away from me, even the comfort of knowing that Mum might know I was there… I looked back at Mum willing her to see me.

Instead, there was the sudden and incessant sound that nobody on earth ever needs to hear, as the machine's audio alarm suddenly screamed out. The shrill, harsh sound of its single note will stay with me forever. The alarm eventually shut down and the sound appeared to die in tandem with my Mother's last involuntary movement. Her eyes half-opened and then froze. A single tear slid down her face, leaving its track through the grey dirt on her white, white skin. It came to settle on the pillow, where it was absorbed into the pure white cotton, leaving a grey smudge in its place. My heart stopped. I couldn't breathe. I became unaware of everything except the smudge on that pillow, and the echo of the alarm in my head. I don't recall my Nan's arm around me, or what happened next. I just knew my life had, at that moment changed forever. I was just seventeen years old.

Saying goodbye to Mum on that September day was one of the hardest things I've ever done and I cried until I ached. I held onto Nan like I couldn't bear to let go. In the forefront of my mind there was still the terrible truth that my Dad had not been found. And for my Nan, to lose her son like this... Well, I couldn't imagine what was going through her mind. We couldn't stay in New York, it was time for us to make necessary arrangements and leave. Knowing we had to leave without seeing my Dad I thought my heart would break. Not seeing Dad had such a profound and lasting effect on me. The thought of never having his strong, hairy arms around me again, or teasing him about the grey hairs appearing at his temples, was almost too much for me to bear. It is almost as if I could not accept that he was dead… especially as I had no proof of this. Of course, I knew he was… I just knew he was. But not having anything physically left of him was the most difficult thing I have ever had to cope with. They now say he was located at the point of impact where the first plane hit, and would have known nothing of the situation. The time and place of his last known location had been confirmed in my Mother's surviving Filofax, which I still have. Those were the facts, but it didn't make the truth any easier to bear.

There was a day, the Thursday after we returned home I think it was, there was a knock at Nan's door. I answered, almost in a daze and when I looked up, the shadow through the glass made me think that Dad had come home! Eagerly I threw the door open, completely prepared to jump into his strong and hugely hairy arms as he would say, "Hi Kookie, I'm home!" Disappointment doesn't even come close to the feeling I experienced when I saw that it wasn't him. I found myself confronted by some freckle-faced youth asking if I wanted… Do you know what? I cannot even recall what he actually wanted. I just remember slamming the door shut in his face and running up to my room and remaining there until Nan came in to see what was wrong. Her comforting arms were not the ones I wished to be in, but they were all I had, and I was more than grateful for that. You see, the thing is, the youth bore no resemblance to my Father's stature at all, which made me realise just how badly I was wishing and wanting it to be him. I still believed that he would walk through the door.

There were more tears as the days turned into weeks, then months. I don't think a night went by without tears before finally the relief of sleep would claim me for a short duration. On occasions, I would watch my own tears pool onto the pillow where they would stay for a moment or two before disappearing. It maybe sounds crazy, but I really felt close to Mum at times like that. As for Dad's absence, I would make up stories about the adventures he was involved in, which explained his being away. I would convince myself that he was in the deepest, darkest parts of the World where he was on a mission to save humanity. In my mind, he would just solve one case, only to be thrown into another. The cases he was solving were so important, that without him, I would not have the freedom I had today. Over time, Dad turned into some sort of Superhero as I endowed him with special powers, whereas, if truth were known, the only superpower I ever wanted from him was the strength to be with me. The strength to hold me and tell me that everything was going to be all right. But as with all Superheroes, this turned out to be fantasy on my part..., just like Finitia.

Eventually I threw myself back into my work. I had no choice. I soon found I had distanced myself from my friends, and occasionally even stayed away from Nanny Rose. I would live to regret that, as once again and unbeknown to me, I would lose her too in a sad and dramatic way.

Chapter 2

Nanny Rose

It is strange, but due to my parents' work, I always seemed to be with Nanny Rose when I was younger. Especially, it would appear, when major things happened. One of the most memorable events was when I was experiencing stomach pains. Being eleven when that happened was one thing, but suffering the indignity of grumbling pains and being told by my peers that it was wind, was completely another. But this wasn't wind, it turned out to be my first period. And it couldn't have happened at a worse time. Or so I thought at the time.

I was due to go on a school trip that day but couldn't face it, so I phoned in sick and cancelled my place. A classmate of little means filled my vacant seat. The process of selection for this type of situation was simple. My parents had already paid for the place on the trip, but there was a shortlist to choose from of those less well-off should someone cancel. Sarah Littlejohn willingly took my place and dutifully claimed my seat on the coach as her own. From what I heard, the trip went well until the return leg. The coach collided with a mobile crane unit, which had suffered a catastrophic tyre failure. The retracted but exposed crane section at the front of the mobile unit caused the most damage to the coach. The impact ripped through the metal as if it were made of wet tissue paper. The only fatality in the event was that of the girl who had taken my place on the trip. Sadness does not go far enough in circumstances like this, and relief seems so callous. Being so young, I just didn't know how to react. So, for some reason and seemingly out of character, I showed little emotion for the loss of Sarah. I suppose I may have detached myself from the reality of realising that that should have been me, and not her. I still think about that day with great sadness.

If it was at all possible, what made this event even more dramatic was that I had thoughtlessly failed to tell Nan that I had swapped my seat that day, as she was out shopping when I made the phone call to school to cancel my place. As far as she was concerned, I was on the coach when it crashed. She obviously panicked when the survivors came back to the school in a fleet of minibuses as she was waiting to pick me up. Her anxiety rose when she became aware that I wasn't on any of the buses. When Nan realised what had happened she felt a rush of relief, shortly followed by a blaze of anger, since she had gone through the terrible stress of not knowing where I was. On the other hand, Sarah's Mother, who was heartbroken, asked Nan why this had happened to her little girl and not to me... It was then that Nan realised how close she had come to losing me.

When I look back to that evening I was absolutely horrified at what I saw when Nan eventually walked into my bedroom. In place of my lively, independent Nan was a confused and extremely old woman, her face crumpled with concern. By now, her angst had turned to relief and happiness in seeing me alive, but it had taken its toll. She had lived through a nightmare, which was to have lasting and underlying consequences.

Nan once told me that she had had a tough upbringing herself, and even before Dad's birth, she'd had to endure a life of drudgery. That was what life was like then. Her youth had been spent looking after her siblings since she, like me, was the only girl in the family. Her Father, a Hotel Porter, could not provide the finest that life could offer, but he did his best. The only treats Nan could expect was when, on occasions, she was told to 'Run something around to your Dad'. Then, she would take him packages of food that her Mother had sneaked into her bag from her kitchen job. Nan told me that she would slip in through the front entrance of the Hotel and seek him out. The Hotel was busy, and being a little girl, she would quietly sneak by the reception area when the opportunity would allow. Her Father would secrete her away and allow her to take her pick from the package she had brought into him. From her vantage point, she could watch the world pass her by whilst wishing she could be part of it all. Seeing the splendour around showed her what she was missing, and she promised herself that when she was older, she would walk through the doors of that very Hotel as a guest. This was never to happen though, since the Hotel was eventually pulled down after suffering heavy bomb damage during the War. Nothing was the same after that, since the symbol that represented her future had so sadly been destroyed.

At the age of 13, in fact on her 13th birthday, she lost both her parents and was taken away to live with a distant relative. I have no details of how she came to lose them, but I fully understand the pain she must have felt at the time. From this point onwards, I knew nothing of her life apart from a few snippets I heard from Mum and Dad about some 'dark secrets'. Nothing made much sense to me about these secrets and Nan would never divulge anything directly to me. It would appear that Nan had a past, but it was always today she lived for.

The day Sarah Littlejohn died turned out to be all about Nan's future, which she thought was lost forever. Thinking that I had died made her realise that she should have done more to prevent it from happening, although, what more she could have done was something well beyond my understanding. This all happened at a time my parents were away on one of their many trips and knew nothing of the events on that day, or ever since. Between Nan and I, we kept it quiet and never discussed it openly again. I was happier to forget that time, although there is little that can help you forget something like that… is there?

When my parents died, I almost resented Sarah for taking my place on that day. My death would have taken me away from all the hurt I now had inside me. I somehow blamed her for all the pent up emotions I still had gnawing at me. I suppose this insulated feeling made it more bearable for me to cope with losing them, but I don't know.

On reflection, I remember more about Sarah's funeral than I did my Mum's. In fact, I remember more about Dad's memorial than I do about Mum's funeral and could never figure that out. Mum's funeral felt like make-believe, and I think I almost detached myself from the day in order to be able to get through it, whereas Sarah's was filled with wailing and sorrow, as relatives and school friends alike shared their grief. I felt so alone being there as I stared at her small white, gold trimmed coffin. On that occasion, Sarah's Mum came up to me and through gritted teeth thanked me for coming. Her Dad, on the other hand had even less to say to me, and through his eyes, I suddenly felt his pain. He had lost his one and only little girl, the little girl who he had doted on. At the time, I could not bring myself to acknowledge his loss, so I merely looked down at my shoes, turned, and left the crematorium, crying tears of self-pity as I left. Once again, I was without my parents' comfort because they were, yet again, away. I only had Nanny Rose to help me through the confusion of it all.

As the years passed, Nanny Rose and I learned how to live with our eventual losses, although Nanny Rose, as usual, kept her deepest feelings well hidden from me.

My twenty-first birthday eventually came and went without much of a fanfare, although I did receive a letter from my parents' solicitor. The letter referred to the conditions of their Will and stated that a sum of six hundred thousand pounds was to be transferred to my account as part of my inheritance from the family trust. The remaining amounts would continue to be managed by a faceless trustee, who would in due course, help accrue interest on the investments my parents had so carefully stipulated. A second and more substantial amount would become available to me when I reached my twenty-fifth birthday. On my twenty-eighth birthday, I was to receive the remaining funds, which by then, would amount to several millions. I knew all about these vast amounts, but I could not have cared less at the time, although the money was soon to play an important part in my life. Indeed, I was given something I thought I would never find; financial freedom… But at what price?

On receiving my inheritance I did two things, the first was to hand in my notice at work! Secondly, I asked the only person I could trust for advice in these matters. I needed guidance on what best to do with the money. Nanny Rose took her time in responding, "Well, I suggest you invest in property, just like I did." Nan was extremely well off in her own right, but I wasn't aware of her prowess in the property market. She later explained, and the explanation gave me a small insight into her previously sheltered life. This is what she said: "After your grandfather died I was left some cash, a property and no debts. The property was Ridgeway House, where you used to visit as a little girl, but I doubt if you would remember it. The house was far too big for me to cope with, so I decided to move to a smaller property. I was about to sell it, when I realised its true potential. I then leased it out, since I projected I would make a lot more money than I would have had I sold it. With the proceeds, I bought more property and so on. With what I made, I helped your Mum and Dad set up their business." She faltered slightly, "Now that I think back, that would have been the reason why they were in New York..." She petered off and turned away without ever finishing the conversation. Although nobody else felt that way, through her reaction, Nan suggested it was her fault. How could she possibly have known they would both die in such horrific circumstances? Nobody ever knows such things. They were in the wrong place at the wrong time, tragically, but I have since convinced myself that in life, things are mapped out... just as in death.

Ridgeway House was a place I knew well, I did indeed remember it, but I never really felt the connection between it and my family. Perhaps this was because I was too young to realise the association, although on reflection, I know I found it creepy. The house, situated near the Thames and within sight of the water, was where we would sometimes picnic as a family. Later in life, I would pass it and deliberately steer away from its shadow. The house, to me, never reflected the beauty or the tranquillity of the location where it so boldly sat.

My grandfather, Nan's husband, was an enigma to me, since nobody ever spoke of him or of his life. In my younger days, I did find a trunk full of clothes, which included a military uniform and a box full of medals. There were also a few photographs of him when he was younger. I found nothing of him in the latter years and leading up to his death. Apart from then, I had not thought of his existence since I never really knew him. Now though, realising how he had looked after Nanny Rose so well, he became a new hero in my life. I conjured up this image of a dashing, moustached officer astride a magnificent steed. He would dash through the enemy lines and cut down the foe with his sabre whilst ignoring the wounds he had received. There was no logic in my fantasy since I didn't know which war was which and never realised that he had, in fact, died in the Second World War.

Sadly, not long after the conversation I had with Nan about her background and wealth and the story of Ridgeway House, Nanny Rose suffered a stroke. Her preliminary recovery was remarkably quick and her resilience was extraordinary. Initially, even her doctors were astounded by her strength to pull through what most would not have done. Nevertheless, the stroke, had taken its toll and she would never be the same again after that. She was restricted to moving around slowly with a walker and spent a lot of time in bed. I am sure it was for this reason that she finally decided enough was enough.

Towards the end of her life, she suffered well beyond what one person should endure. Throughout this, her kindness to humanity showed no bounds. In those instances, it manifested itself in her making other people feel comfortable in her presence, even when it was known that she was in extreme pain. She had an ability to switch emphasis from her own discomfort, into a more positive subject. Within no time at all, she would have you believe she was feeling better, even though I knew she wasn't. If, however, she asked you how *you* were, then she expected an honest answer and listened with unparalleled intensity.

Throughout this time and by way of preparing me for what was to come, she would often say things like, 'I hope they have warmer weather in the next world' or 'When I get to the next world I want to be able to get up without saying ouch!' Her favourite though, was 'Gramps must wonder what is taking me so long to get to him. I know he won't settle 'til I get there.' Some of what she said was strange to me and sometimes spoken in a voice I did not recognise. It was at times like these that she would repeat herself over and over again. The only real words I ever caught during the latter part of this period were 'Mercy' and 'Forgive' and even then, I wasn't quite sure about the 'Mercy' bit. There was peace just before she died, though. And then she muttered something almost incoherent. I rolled her words around in my mind and eventually understood enough to know what she had said, "I'll say hello to them all for you." I smiled and stroked her hair for the last time.

She finally 'left this world', as she used to call it, for the 'next' precisely on the fourth anniversary of what is now known as 9/11. Ironically, yes, she died on the same day as her son, only separated by four short years.

Nanny Rose left many things behind… sadness, happiness, positive thought, great memories…, and a huge pot of money. I had shared all of the emotions she displayed, since I had spent most of my life in her care. I was able to cry for her knowing truly what I was crying for. With Mum and Dad's deaths I had so many conflicting emotions; huge loss but anger too, and when Sarah died I felt confused and detached, but with Nanny Rose, I had one emotion; utter relief. Towards the end Nanny Rose's life, we both felt like we were in purgatory. I hated to see her suffer, as much as she hated me to see her suffer. Individually, we both knew there would only be one peaceful outcome… her own death.

And so it was that I laid her to rest.

My Nanny Rose.

Chapter 3

First Contact

As crazy as this sounds, the day after Nanny Rose died I sought solace in my computer and was immediately annoyed by a series of 'pop-ups'. My multifaceted security system should have protected me against events like this. Even a detailed diagnostic of my computer could not recover enough information for me to pinpoint the problem. I felt nothing but frustration from this persistent and uninvited intrusion. No matter how hard I tried, and believe me I tried everything, I could not stop one particular site from returning. I even began to doubt my own technical abilities in fixing the problem. This, for me, was a first. My firewall, pop-up blocker and security system, all appeared to be failing me… And I had the best.

An internet search based on the information I had revealed nothing, although the site itself seemed innocuous and somehow unthreatening. Nothing I did would reveal the source of site, or its owner. Irony has its moments and my nickname Cookie seemed so inappropriate in this instance. A domain search offered no new leads in how the site was infiltrating my maximised security system. My system did not flag up any threats related to its manifestation or to its origin. After hours of trying to eradicate the site, I actually stopped and looked at the content: ***'www.oneforrosecottage.com'***. This was something I had not come across before, so I 'hedged my bets' and isolated it before opening the site fully. Once again, my system did not see it as a threat and another check revealed there were no viruses, Trojans, or other nasties for me to encounter or to worry about.

The site, ***'www.oneforrosecottage.com'***, itself, was for an online auction house, advertising nothing other than a charming thatched cottage located in the described 'sleepy' village of Pitton. Instead of instantly trying to delete the information, I found myself riveted by the brief online description of the property, which seemed ideal and inviting. Armed with the information I had gleaned, I tried to search for more details and became thrown by my computer as it once again teased me with its inability to react to my instructions. Each time I sought new information, the page would refresh and return to the original site.

In frustration, I left home to visit a local internet café situated at the end of the street. With a skinny latte in hand, I prepared myself to use one of the many machines available to me. I selected one near the window and sat with complete confidence that I would now solve the mystery. After all, this particular computer had no connection to mine. My idea was to choose a system that was as remotely detached from my problems as I could. Here, I was able to enter the name and all of the details I had to hand, which let's face it, wasn't much.

Once again, I encountered all sorts of extreme problems. These complications manifested themselves in all sorts of ways. On occasions, the search engine would direct me away from the general information section and onto images. This enforced method of search threw up all sorts of grotesque pictures. They centred mainly on scenes of death and destruction. They included vehicle crashes, war scenes and pictures of the 9/11aftermath. Every picture that flashed across the screen appeared to have a vague connection to me. At least, that's how I saw it. The last scene to flash up was that of a damaged coach. This scene revealed its shredded insides due to a large gash running along the whole length of the vehicle. The computer then crashed.

I could take no more and stood up abruptly, spilling my coffee onto the keyboard. Not wanting to hang about or explain my actions, I ran out of the café in tears.

Why? I asked myself. Why was this happening and why was it happening now when I already had so much to deal with? Perhaps I should leave well alone I thought, before deciding I would go straight home and format my computer. Yes, I always backed up my system and had nothing of value to lose but my sanity. I was now determined to obliterate all of the images I had just seen; by symbolically obliterating the reason I had seen them in the first place.

The process of formatting the hard drive is relatively simple but for some reason my computer put up a fight. It was a fight I had to win since there was no reason a computer should deny a direct command. Furthermore, I was 'Queen' of the cybernet, and no machine was going to get the better of me! At last, I had total control and pressed the last button of command. I watched with perverted pleasure as the computer finally succumbed to a path of total annihilation. From here on in, I was convinced I would regain full control of my computer and thus, my world.

How wrong could I be?

Reformatted and reloaded with trusted software and programs, I beefed up my security and felt satisfied I had done enough. I confidently entered cyberspace with aplomb and enjoyed a days' surfing, whilst catching up with my many outstanding e-mails. I briefly shut down the system so I could enjoy a well-earned takeaway with thoughts of triumph, but the computer had other ideas. Before long, I was back exactly where I started, as suddenly ***'www.oneforrosecottage.com'*** appeared, yet again.

I put up with this persistent intrusion for another three weeks before I felt enough was enough, and decided it was time to give Joel a call.

Chapter 4

Joel

Joel was an interesting character to say the least, and one I was more than pleased to know.

There are only a few things left in life that are important to me and currently being without a boyfriend is not one of them, since most of my ex's were arseholes and only after one thing. Give a man a smile and it is all he could do to control himself in the trouser department. Accept a drink from him and he thinks he owns you. No! That's not for me! Perhaps it's because I think more like a man, which somehow gives me an advantage in certain situations. I can for instance, see life from their point of view, but have always wondered why we, the women of the world, still accept their bullshit. We all deserve better than that, so why do we do it? Don't get me wrong, I've been there too, and I am still awaiting the right man, but enough is enough. I've also been in situations, which I am not so proud of and here's the rub… I now feel I can do without them, especially since my most recent and devastating loss.

There is though, one exception to the my aforementioned opinion of men. His name is Joel and is three years older than I am. We were at junior school together and were friends from the start, although initially I had to admire him from afar. By this, I mean I first saw him from a distance on the way to school and liked what I saw. His blonde tousled hair was the first thing I noticed about him, followed by his bright, vibrant blue eyes and lofty slim features. Some could describe him as being pretty, since his face was the most symmetrical I have ever seen, but to me it had nothing to do with looks. I suppose, my 'crush' on him really started when I had my dinner money stolen by some local hooligans. Seeing what happened, he bravely chased off the bullies and ended up sharing his lunch with me. From then on, Joel was always with me in everything I did. It was he who would eventually push me into computers and computer games such as Doom, Diablo and Warcraft. The games alone were not enough for me, since I wanted to know how they were put together. Yes, very unlike a regular girl in that sense…, but that's another story!

Nevertheless, Joel would eventually break my heart and far from being mad at him, I all of a sudden realised just what a fantastic friend he was. You see, I always teased him, flirted with him, and once even asked him out on a date, but to no avail. It was soon after that occasion he told me, in extreme confidence, that he was gay! He further explained that at first he thought he was only going through a 'phase'. This so-called 'phase' was to end in dramatic fashion when he realised his feelings for another friend, Andy Turnbull, were more than just friendship. But, Andy was not gay, and the subsequent confession was end in conflict when Joel hesitantly revealed his true feelings.

Andy dropped Joel like a 'hot potato' and ended up causing him long term trouble, which manifested itself in something akin to a personal vendetta. This vendetta was in the form of persecution, which sometimes ended up being physical... And not in the physical way that Joel would have liked.

It was then, that our roles reversed and I became his protector. Although I am not too proud of what I did, I relentlessly teased Andy and somehow turned the tables on him. I spread malicious rumours about him, which seemed to be believed. These rumours centred on the falsehood that he exposed himself to me, and that I was less than impressed by what I saw. Although not true, the taunting he endured went far beyond what I had expected but, somehow, I didn't seem to care. The final insult came when I hacked into his computer and stole his identity. I 'toyed' with his life and manipulated it without mercy until he finally left the scene. What happened to him I don't know.

From then on, school got better and better, since Joel and I shared everything. Homework was made easier by the mere fact that my specialist subjects were not Joel's and visa-versa. Here, we excelled and always came out on top. I guess being so well attuned to each other had its benefits. There was nothing to get in the way of our friendship, and definitely no tacky moments to spoil our fun.

Since Nan's passing, I was staying at her home, as I felt so uncomfortable at my parents' house. I suppose I still felt uneasy knowing she and Dad would never be coming back to it. The other reason I felt more relaxed at Nan's, was because it was there that I spent most of my 'growing up' time.

Although we had frequently spoken on the phone, I had not seen Joel since Nan's funeral. For now though, I awaited his presence with the anxiety of an expectant Father! The closer the time came to his arrival the more anxious and excited I became. I paced the floor and occasionally walked over to my computer to see if I could make a difference to the display, but to no avail. From the computer, I paced to the window and so on until I knew I had to get a grip on my sanity. As usual, in times of extreme anxiety, I relaxed by pouring myself a glass of my favourite wine.

Joel arrived on schedule, since he hated tardiness. His less than flamboyant entrance reflected his tiredness from a long and arduous trip. The enforced trip to Manchester from London was due to work, which meant he'd had to stay over the weekend and well beyond what he thought was reasonable. Although eager to resolve my frustrating computer problem, and to have a good cry in his arms about Nanny Rose and my parents, I considered his weariness and I decided to let him relax. He showered and emerged from the bathroom wearing my fluffy and oversized dressing gown. His mischievous, cheesy grin told me he felt comfortable enough to finally sit down and relax with an obligatory large glass of red wine. Within minutes, we were talking about our respective weekends... Correction, Joel talked about his weekend.

After a second glass of wine and in Joel's company, my mood had lightened considerably.

Amidst the giggles and laughter, Joel told me about his Saturday night with his newfound friend, Aaron. Aaron sounded like a dream, but our laughter centred on Aaron's only failing. You see, Joel is a natural born dancer, whereas, Aaron couldn't dance at all. Joel got up and re-enacted some of the moves to give me some idea of what he had to contend with on the night. I wasn't sure if Joel was exaggerating the moves but they were funny, made more so by the fact he was wearing my ridiculously huge dressing gown. There was a moment of reflection though, as Joel paused to say that his reactions to what he saw as funny had hurt Aaron's feelings, and after that, there was no going back. They parted on a sour note as Aaron stormed off whilst Joel tried, to no avail, to placate the situation. Joel's final note on the subject was that of regret, since he felt he had failed in yet another relationship. In this instance, he had been made to feel like it was mainly due to his associated lack of compassion and tactlessness. Of all the people I knew, I could honestly say that Joel had never let me down. Furthermore, it was not usually in his nature to outwardly embarrass people or belittle them, so hearing the story made me realise how bad he must have felt afterwards. If anything, I knew he would do anything to make amends, but in this case, there was nothing he could do about it.

The subject eventually turned to how I was coping since the loss of Nanny Rose, as well as my parents. Here, Joel excelled in his ability to comfort me in my many times of need. He knew exactly when to say the right thing, and what to say, coupled with just the right amount of warm hugs. Then, as was usual these days, we came to discuss 9/11 and what has become known as the 'Sarah Littlejohn Incident'. Somehow, we always came to this point in any of our profound discussions. We both reflected on these subjects for a while before Joel broke the silence, "Hey girl, tell me what is on your mind. You sounded serious on the phone."

I turned to the table situated behind the sofa we were sitting on, and pulled my laptop towards me causing a pile of paperwork to cascade onto the floor, "Shit! I just knew that was going to happen." I said before adding, "I need your advice on something. Something I thought I could handle." I opened the computer before thrusting it onto his lap.

Joel studied the computer with an analytical eye, "What am I looking at? I mean is there something I should be looking at in particular?"

With his questions still ringing in my ears I unceremoniously leant over, snatched the computer from his hands, and stared at my usual humdrum home page. There was nothing there to suggest what I had seen earlier. In view of this, I opened the history tab and stared in total disbelief. There was nothing to be seen! There were no references to suggest I was ever on the offending page, so I typed ***'www.oneforrosecottage.com'*** into the search engine. Blank… nothing… nada! With my sanity at stake, I tried every combination available to me before giving up in total frustration.

Throughout this time, a concerned looking Joel was quietly observing me. He never openly doubted me but I wondered at the time, if he thought I was finding Nan's recent loss a reason for my strange behaviour.

Joel silently rose from his seat and picked up the papers strewn across the floor, before returning to me with the remaining few drops from our once full bottle of Australian Shiraz, "I think you had better tell me what I was supposed to see before we go on."

I agreed and with one swift flick of the wrist I recklessly threw my laptop onto the adjacent armchair, "Well, I suppose I should start by telling you that I think somebody has hacked into my computer." This snippet of information astounded Joel since he knew of my extreme capabilities and prowess on a computer. Furthermore, Joel had originally exceeded in this field, until I overtook him with my natural technology skills. Joel then asked for all the relevant details. From there, we pieced together everything that we learned. Using this information, we retrieved the computer and searched the web by typing in the only word other than Rose Cottage that I could remember from the site - the word 'Pitton'.

The results were, at first, deemed disappointing. However, given the parameters, I was pleased since we came up with two worthy results. It stated 'Pitton and Farley, near Salisbury and Pitton, Gower Peninsula in Wales.' For some reason I typed in the latter location first since the locality felt right for the type of cottage I had seen. The result excited me since two things stood out. Firstly, there was Rose Cottage and secondly, perhaps rather strangely, the cottage was situated in Ridgeway Close. The tentative association between Rose Cottage and the name Ridgeway, which originally had links to my Nan, had me buzzing. For some unknown reason, I felt there was a connection, until I saw a picture of the cottage in question. The beautiful double fronted slate tile roofed building was not what I expected to see. I was certain I would see the older looking thatched cottage I had previously glimpsed on my laptop. Disappointed, I searched every conceivable photographic angle I could, but to no avail. Exhausting this particular site was very disheartening since, by now, I felt there was a meaningful reason why I should have been looking there. I swore out of frustration, "Bugger!" Then I exclaimed, "Why can't I find the site that I want to now?" Disheartened, I no longer felt the urgent need to expose the glitches in my computer.

Once again, I carelessly discarded my laptop.

Wine and Joel's company was my only solace now.

Chapter 5

Revelations

After a while, I picked up the computer on the off chance that something would reveal itself to me. Nothing in my second search jumped out at me and for this reason, I suggested we call it a night.

Joel was pleased to be given an opportunity to 'turn in', since by now he was shattered. This, combined with his fair share of a second bottle of red, had taken its toll. I too, felt the need to sleep and initially bid Joel goodnight as we left for our respective bedrooms. There was always room at Nanny Rose's for Joel, especially as they always got on so well with each other. Many a time, as early teenagers, we would have 'sleep-overs', which would be the highlight of any weeknight. These events were liberating, since we would often share details about what we knew of the people we liked and disliked. I knew I could discuss anything with him from the changes in puberty, to sex and even make-up without the fear of conflict.

We finally said goodnight on the landing before going our separate ways. As usual, I placed my laptop on my bedroom desk before having a wash, brushing my teeth and slipping into my comfy PJs. By the time I got into bed, I was as near to sleep as I could get without the sandman knowing. The night seemed short and the light in the room indicated to me that it was time to get up. I was more than a little surprised when I realised the only source of light in my room was coming from my laptop, which I distinctly remember both turning off and closing the lid. As I looked at the screen, it changed from a brightly lit background to the more recent elusive ***'www.oneforrosecottage.com'***. I banged my elbow on my bedside table in an effort to get to the computer in the hopes it would not change away from its current page. This rap on my elbow was enough for me to know that I wasn't dreaming. I lifted the laptop and cradled it in the crook of my left arm whilst I studied the content. As I searched the page for a little bit more information about the site, something else grabbed my attention. The name *Alexander P Glasspool* and a telephone number appeared under a separate heading that wasn't there before.

I looked down to the bottom right hand side of the screen, which revealed the time to be half past two in the morning. Not only was it still dark outside, I had only been in bed for an hour or so. Now fully awake I decided to do some more digging and entered the name Alexander P Glasspool into my search engine. A very business-like and professional looking site came up immediately, headed 'Glasspool Auction House, Salisbury in the Beautiful County of Wiltshire.' Surprisingly, there was a defined link between the search I did before I went to bed and what I was looking at now. The link in this instance was in the form of a single word... that word was *Pitton*. Suddenly it all became clear to me. This much was clear; the mention of Pitton and Farley near Salisbury, was far too much of a coincidence for them not to be connected. I immediately rang the telephone number shown on the screen. I did this for no other reason than for proof of its very existence.

The phone rang six times before an answer machine kicked into life. The recorded message of a rather plum-voiced man came back, "*You have reached the offices of Glasspool Auction House. I am sorry I am not available to take your call...*" I put the phone down and my heart leapt expectantly, knowing now I was not going mad or imagining the existence of the mysterious site. This feeling was short lived as I then began to doubt the connection, since a quick search of Glasspool's site revealed no mention of Rose Cottage. Remarkably, from that moment onwards, I would never see the Rose Cottage site again. It was as if by establishing the existence of Alexander P Glasspool, I had found the right means to eliminate the site. On the other hand, I now had a new lead to follow. Then I thought about the logic of what had been plaguing me for the last few weeks. My thoughts centred on one simple word… WHY!

I couldn't sleep, in both anticipation of Joel's awakening and the excitement of telling him what I had found. He awoke to find me anxiously sitting on the end of his bed, "Jeez you scared me! How long have you…?"

I didn't let him finish his sentence as I explained what I had found. What I didn't tell him was how I came to be looking at my computer so deep into the night. That would come later.

For now though, we spoke about other things when all of a sudden Joel acted strangely before announcing that he 'needed to pee'. I lounged on Joel's bed as he grabbed his phone and went to the bathroom. Whilst he was gone, I climbed into the warmth of his bed before slipping into a light sleep. After about an hour or so, I awoke with a start to find Joel still missing. Guessing he had gone downstairs, I searched, only to find him sitting on the sofa still in his nightwear and staring at the static screen of my television. I touched him gently on the arm, which brought him into life, "Jeez, will you stop doing that! That's twice this morning you have made me jump." I apologised seconds before he burst out laughing, "Hey Claire, thanks for everything. I mean thanks for being a friend. Boy, have I got a hangover and a headache to prove it."

I merely smiled and went into the kitchen to make fresh coffee for us both as I anticipated my next move.

Over breakfast, I anxiously eyed the clock and the telephone in equal measures, "Oh come on!" I muttered out aloud. At the stroke of nine, I dialled the last digit of the telephone number I had written down, and soon found myself talking to none other than Alexander P Glasspool.

"Good morning, Alexander Glasspool speaking. How can I help you?" He said softly

I almost hung up and wished I had prepared myself better, "Oh! Um, I am enquiring about Rose Cottage."

"Rose Cottage…?" His voice petered off before repeating what he had just said, "Rose Cottage!" He seemed to clear his throat, "I'm sorry I don't understand. How…? What do you know about Rose Cottage?"

"Well you see..." I faltered too, not knowing how to explain myself so I became slightly defensive and lied, "Um, well you see a friend of mine told me about it. And..." I was prevented from completing my sentence.

Glasspool's voice seemed a little strained, "Friend? I would be surprised at that, since the cottage in question has only just been handed over to me by the trustees of the late Miss Mabel Adams estate."

Hearing this I thought I had made a grave mistake by phoning and was about to hang up when I suddenly regained my composure, "I am sorry Mr Glasspool. I guess that me knowing that you have a property of that name appears to be more important to you than selling it."

Somehow, my nerve had outstripped his and he appeared to drop his inquisitive attitude, "I am sorry Miss er..." He paused slightly in the hopes that I would reveal my name but I felt confident enough to make him wait. He continued, "...Well Miss. Apparently, the previous agents acting on behalf of the executors have had extreme trouble in selling the property. You see, it has been on the market for several years and to my knowledge, very few people have ever viewed the property until now. Perhaps you are mistaking this property for another, although I must admit, I am rather intrigued by your call."

There was a distinct change in Mr Glasspool's attitude so I firmly took hold of the situation, "My name is Miss Chambers, Miss Claire Chambers." I now felt assertive, "Look, I am interested in viewing the cottage and I am prepared to come down from London to view it. Perhaps later today?" I said this without thinking what Joel might say or even considering the travelling implications.

By now, Mr Glasspool had also regained his former composure, "Very well, you can view the property. However, I already have a series of appointments related to the property. These appointments cover the best part of this morning. So, shall we say three thirty this afternoon? Do you have an e-mail address where I can send you the details and a map?" He didn't wait for me to answer before adding, "By the way, I think it is worth mentioning that I am obliged to sell this property at auction. So, unless you are the only bidder I cannot promise anything. I have just sent details to a few of my most regular clientele who I know will have an interest in this sort of property. Oh, one other thing. The map will not show the location of the property but that of a local hostelry where we can meet. The property is a little out of the way and can be difficult to reach."

Without consultation, I willingly gave my e-mail address and agreed the time and location before saying goodbye. I put the phone down and looked across the table at Joel, who was throwing all sorts of exasperated expressions my way. I expected a barrage of questions and recriminations but I should have known better, "Hell yeah. You go girl. I hope he said yes. I could do with a trip to… Uh, where exactly are we going? Never mind, get yourself ready, we're off on a road trip." He jumped up, "Yee Ha!" Was his final response, to which I merely smiled.

Within the hour, we were in Joel's VW Golf and on our way down the M3 corridor and heading towards Wiltshire. By us 'not so carefully' following the map that Mr Glasspool had sent us, we eventually arrived at the Silver Plough, in Pitton, just in time for lunch. We would have arrived sooner but Joel had taken several wrong turns before eventually finding the right road. Despite his sexual orientation, he sported one annoying male trait. By not listening to his co-driver or asking for directions, we added at least thirty miles to our trip.

There was, however, something amiss with Joel's recent attitude, although I was unable to pinpoint exactly what it was. The closer we got to our destination the more he seemed preoccupied and distant. I put this down to tiredness, after all, he had

had a rough night, and to add to his already 'full' weekend, he had an earlier start than he had expected.

We entered the bar where we were greeted by an eclectic mix of faces and characters. The place went extremely quiet as we ventured in and the silence was only broken by a booming voice coming from a friendly looking face from behind the bar, "Hello you two. Welcome to our Inn. My name is Stephen and this is my wife Susan." He directed his gaze to a woman to his left and standing slightly in the background. Although all eyes were still on us, the patrons then commenced talking… some in hushed tones.

With a friendly smile, Stephen's wife Susan, then stepped forward and spoke, "And what brings you to our neck of the woods?"

My response was chirpy to say the least, "Oh, just meeting up with somebody to do with a local property. Rose Cottage, do you know it?"

The reaction to my question was somewhat disproportionate, and akin to somebody committing a carnal act on the carpet in front of them. There was then a mix of loud sighs and unguarded responses to what I had just said.

Stephen grinned, "Don't mind them Miss, they are just having a joke at your expense." With that, he shot a threatening glance at a white bearded man sitting to our left. The man grudgingly nodded and everybody continued with the various things they were doing when we arrived.

Joel nudged me and gave out a nervous giggle as I dared to ask the next question, "Do you know Rose Cottage then?"

Susan's answer was sweet but concise, "No." She looked nervously at Stephen who just shook his head before adding, "Still getting our feet under the table. Anyhow, do you wish to order a drink, or see today's menu perhaps?" The question was almost an invitation for me to change the subject to which I gratefully accepted in light of the earlier responses.

I looked around as if to find something positive to talk about and spied something of interest, "Ted Heath drank here!" I exclaimed. What had prompted me to say such a thing was the sight of a brass plaque attached to the back of a cushion-strewn bench almost opposite my chair. It stated, 'SIR EDWARD HEATH'S FAVOURITE SEAT'.

Joel threw me a bemused look, "Who on earth is Sir Edward Heath when he is at home?"

Both Stephen and Susan laughed nervously but it was left for me to explain, "Ted Heath! Morning Cloud! Number ten Downing Street! Don't you know your Prime Ministers?"

Joel's impish response proved he knew exactly who I had been referring too from the start, "Oh, *THAT* Edward Heath!" The emphasis placed on the word 'that' by Joel was followed by a roll of his eyes. I couldn't explain what was happening, but ever since Joel arrived here, he'd started to act strangely. His overly waggish and playful manner in front of others seemed alien to me and totally out of character. Normally, he would only act like this if we were alone, although there was one memorable exception that took place in London many years ago. I'll probably come to that later.

In the meanwhile, we still had time to kill, so we planned to eat our lunch at a leisurely pace whilst restricting ourselves to non-alcoholic drinks. The varied and adventurous food menu offered a better range than we were used to. Unfortunately, our own 'local' only catered for those interested in microwaved meals. We placed our order and felt more at ease as we awaited the culinary delights.

Given the initial and unnerving response to the mere mention of Rose Cottage, I felt loathed to ask any more questions. Despite this, I felt I had an underlying right to know more about the reasons behind the perceived hostilities towards us and was intrigued to know more. Joel, on the other hand seemed to revel in making the people around us squirm. It was almost as if he had read my mind and without deliberation, he called out, "Hey Keep! Do you have a map or something like that so we can see if we can find the cottage for ourselves?"

Although polite, the response was once again negative but the bearded man made a point of downing his Dominos mid-game and left. The rest of the people around him soon followed. Joel merely shrugged as I cringed before nudging him. I felt awkward and slightly ashamed by my companion's lack of manners and restraint.

Something in Joel was indeed greatly amiss.

Resigned to having no other clientele to serve, Stephen and Susan poured themselves a glass of wine and joined us at our table. Stephen spoke first, "Sorry about that, but I guess you can tell that the locals are a touch sensitive about certain subjects, and I also guess that Rose Cottage is one of them. We've only been here a while, and I am as confused as you by their reaction. I'm sure they will come back sometime soon with an apology." He paused slightly and looked at Susan, "Um, I'm sorry. I must confess to misleading you earlier..." He stopped talking and leant forward before continuing in a much-lowered voice, "...You see I... that is, we have heard that the place you speak of has been up for sale for a long time. Apparently, there have been people interested in the property over the years but mostly that has come to nought."

Before he could continue and wanting more information, I suddenly asked a barrage of questions, "Why do you think it has been so hard to sell? Has anybody been here recently to view it? Is there a problem with it? Is it falling down or something like that?"

Cautiously, Stephen backed away a little before starting to answer some of my questions just as Joel made a point of adding, "What she really wants to know is, is it haunted?" This was a consideration I had not made and had me wondering why Joel had mentioned it. I looked at him incredulously, and noted that his appearance was that of a drunk. Although this was not possible, Joel exhibited a marked change in his demeanour and had by now, slumped backwards in his seat.

Stephen looked astonished at Joel's candour as Susan uncomfortably started to answer, "Well it is not for us to say, but you see we understand there is a connection between..."

Her answer remained unfinished as the door to the Inn opened loudly and in walked a person I could only assume to be Alexander P Glasspool. His physique and attire matched the image I had in my head of the Estate Agent cum Auctioneer. He was smartly dressed in a navy blue three-piece suit, light blue shirt and sported a plain mustard-yellow-coloured tie. He was fractionally taller than I had imagined and exhibited a distinguished grey beard. He approached us without hesitation as I quickly looked at my watch. Surely there had been a mistake, my watch showed that he was more than two hours early.

I stood as Joel lolloped in his seat, "Mr Glasspool I presume."

As I spoke, Stephen and Susan got up and left the table, while the man before me watched them closely before answering, "Yes, indeed. Forgive me for my intrusion but I think you have some questions to answer young lady."

His response baffled me, although at the back of my mind I did recall telling him that a friend had tipped me off about the property being for sale. Perhaps he wanted to know who had let out such sensitive and secret information. However, this was plainly not his main concern, "I have just had a strange telephone call to say that you were already here. The female caller told me that you were asking questions about Rose Cottage. Understandable perhaps, but my main concern is why all of my appointments for this morning were no shows? Each and every client has either phoned in to say that they were no longer interested, or failed to show at all. Now, what do you know of this?"

My reaction to this accusation, if that's what it was, was confusion. I desperately tried to convince him that I had nothing to do with his predicament. I even felt aggrieved and suddenly questioned my own motives for following the mysterious links that led me to where I now found myself. Looking around to Joel offered no means of support, since he was now fast asleep with his head slumped forward. With a slightly aggressive tone I responded, "Mr Glasspool, I have no idea what you are talking about. My friend and I..." I threw another furtive look towards Joel, which confirmed I was still on my own, "We left London as soon I received your e-mail giving us directions to where we are now standing. We had been on the road since then, and only arrived here about half an hour ago. So you see, I couldn't possibly have been in a position to interfere with your viewings. Furthermore..." I couldn't think of a 'furthermore' to add to my sentence, so was glad when Mr Glasspool offered a smile and his hand as means of an apology.

After accepting such a warm apology, I offered to buy Mr Glasspool a drink to which he accepted, "A glass of Pinot if you don't mind. Er, is your friend all right?"

With that, I kicked the base of Joel's chair. This stirred him into life, "Oh, is it time already? Can you smell toffee?" He quipped before embarrassingly looking around the room.

Once again, Joel was acting strangely, so I asked Stephen if he could get Mr Glasspool a large Pinot and to add it to my tab. I then grabbed Joel by the arm and led him from the room and out into the car park, "Joel, are you all right? You have been acting rather peculiar since you got up this morning."

Joel rubbed his eyes and looked around before staring at me in total disbelief, "Where in fuck's name are we? Claire, what in the hell is going on? I don't even remember getting out of bed this morning, let alone getting to... Where in the hell are we again?"

In all of the years I had known him, Joel had been my rock. Apart from when he was being persecuted by Andy Turnbull, I knew I could rely on him for both support and companionship. Here though, I felt isolated. I sought out a bench and asked Joel to sit before asking what he last remembered, "Do you have a clue why we are here Joel? Do you remember anything about this morning or Rose Cottage?"

It was as if a light bulb had come on in his head, "Rose Cottage! Yes, that was it! I was visiting you at Rose Cottage. It's right over there you know." He pointed, "Just beyond the school and on the edge of Pitton Copse."

This was not something I was usually prone to, but hearing what he had to say made me feel scared. Joel added, "I'm sorry Claire, but I feel so tired because of all the weekend travelling. Perhaps I should go back to sleep." As soon as he finished his sentence though, he stood bolt upright before reverting to the old Joel I have always loved and respected. There was a peculiar twist in his response, however… "Hi Claire, are you okay? Look, if when we get inside the pub you feel that you want to change your mind and go back home then that's fine by me. I mean, if this guy ever turns up then I shall be with you one hundred per cent. Maybe somebody in there knows where the cottage is…"

Realising Joel had not been fully aware of what had been going on I put my finger to his lips, "Don't worry Joel you're here with me, that's what is important."

We went back into the pub and were cordially greeted by the only three people in there. Joel looked at me in a befuddled way and said, "Have you been here before Claire?" I reassured him all was well and ordered him his favourite tipple, "Rum and coke for my friend over here please, Stephen. He's just feeling a little jet lagged."

Without further questions, Joel sat down and nursed his drink, a look of intense confusion on his face.

Chapter 6

Rose Cottage

After some fine dining and ensuing pleasantries, I agreed to follow Mr Glasspool to our destination. Given Joel's recent 'lapses' I decided that I would drive, and followed Mr Glasspool's brand new, dark green Super Eight Daimler. As we ventured further into the countryside, the Daimler slowed as both sides of the car were becoming perilously close to the hedgerow.

En route, I asked Joel how he was feeling and he responded positively, "Never felt better my friend." He said confidently. Then I asked what he remembered of the day so far, "What a strange question. Oh well, you always have a good reason for asking these things so, um, let me see. What was the question again? Oh, yes! I remember you waking me up this morning and telling me that you had a lead, then I went back to sleep. I also remember arriving at the pub, and being surprised that you knew everybody there. I must admit I was a little confused by that but hey, what a weekend I've had. Perhaps I fell asleep when you were driving us down."

I wanted to tell him that it was 'he' who had driven 'me' but felt deep down it would be best left alone for now. I somehow felt reassured that Joel was not aware of his recent hiatus, as I inwardly knew there was something seriously wrong. I asked him one final question, "Do you remember telling me you knew where Rose Cottage was?"

His answer was short and simple, "Dah, as if I would know where it was."

Mr Glasspool's car rounded a bend and braked suddenly as a herd of errant sheep confronted him. Given the narrow space between his car and the surrounding foliage, I was amazed to see the sheep fight to get past. There was a blare from his horn as the agitated sheep suddenly decided to do something very unexpected, and even more remarkable. Apart from two ewes who had managed to squeeze through a narrow gap beside the car, the rest suddenly jumped in a complete state of panic onto Mr Glasspool's car and clambered over, only to surround ours. Joel let out a scream as one of them got onto its hind legs and stared at us through the window. Instead of passing us, they surrounded the car and caused it to rock from side to side. The sound of bleating increased to a crescendo, leaving Joel pleading with me to do something. I was at a total loss as to what to do so I mirrored Mr Glasspool and leant on the horn.

Now, I am not used to the countryside but I knew enough to know that this type of behaviour was not normal. Each and every animal was staring into the car, and some appeared to be shuffling for a better position to get a better look at the occupants, namely us!

There was the sudden sound of a sharp whistle, which had a remarkable effect on the sheep, as they suddenly turned in unison and walked away as if nothing had happened. Two sheepdogs appeared out of nowhere and took up their respective positions, although it appeared the sheep did not need cajoling to get to their final destination. I used the mirror to look beyond the flock, to see a tall man dressed from head to foot in green combat gear and sporting a flat cap. It appeared from my perspective, that the well-used cap had been deliberately tilted far enough forward to cover his face from view. Mr Glasspool pulled his car forwards a few metres to a position where he could open his door and was out of his car as soon as it stopped. He shouted at the man who just stood his ground, and waited for the last sheep to pass him by, then turned and followed without responding. Soon it was all over, and all that was left in their wake was a trail of wool hanging from some of the barbed branches of the many blackberry bushes to our left and right… And one very angry looking Mr Glasspool. He rushed towards our car in an effort to reach the man in combat clothing. Although the gaps either side of Joel's VW were sufficient enough to allow the sheep to get through, Mr Glasspool couldn't. Despite this, he tried his hardest, but still couldn't wriggle through. His anger was evident, and looking at his car, I could understand why. The newly polished car had been reduced to a pitted mass of small dents and scratches. As well as having a cracked windscreen, one of the wing mirrors had broken off and was hanging down by just a few wires.

I looked around to see that Joel had physically gone to pieces over the incident, whereas I remained remarkably calm. I leaned over to comfort him as he muttered, "It was in their eyes! Did you see their eyes?" He sobbed uncontrollably as I considered my next move.

Given the series of events leading up to our arrival, I seriously contemplated turning around and heading straight for the M3. However, the calling I had to see Rose Cottage was now even stronger than before, so I decided to venture forward, even if I was alone and damn the consequences.

With Joel and Mr Glasspool calmed enough for us to continue, we once more headed down the road. The previously immaculate Daimler indicated right and turned onto a stretch of un-surfaced road. I followed and could imagine the look on Mr Glasspool's face, as his car bounced around on the rough surface.

Soon, the road evened out, which must have made Mr Glasspool happier. As we rounded a second corner, Rose Cottage came into view. On seeing it for the first time, I knew the trip had been worthwhile… despite the stressed state of the two men with me.

The cottage pleased the eye and was all I had expected it to be, and stood out beautifully in the afternoon light. It was picture perfect! There were roses of many colours on both sides of the front door, which itself was enclosed by a small wooden porch. The thatched roof was greyer than the golden colour I had expected it to be, although there were patches of gilded straw to be seen in one particular area. The frontage was mostly symmetrical although the two upstairs windows did not exactly match. The right hand window was slightly askew, almost as if a drunken workman had put it in. I thought this feature was rather endearing and gave the 'cockeyed' face of the house a charming finish. Apart from the white framed windows, the remaining exposed paintwork was bright primrose. The combined colours were made even more vivid by the sun streaming down upon us. The white picket fence bordering the frontage appeared to me, to be freshly painted. Although, on closer inspection there were areas in need of attention and had recently been painted over to hide a blemish or two.

Going through the front door, Mr Glasspool led us into the immediate gloom of the interior. Don't get me wrong, the house was far from gloomy, it was just the contrast of coming in from the outside brightness. Inside was smaller than the exterior had led me to believe it would be, perhaps due to the extreme thickness of the walls. The truncated ceilings and exposed beams gave the lower rooms an air of extreme cosiness, although in some places the feeling was somewhat claustrophobic. The room we were in, I guess, was the lounge or 'parlour' as Nanny Rose would say. Mr Glasspool and Joel were soon left in my wake as I ventured forth, and both seemed happy to leave me to get on and explore.

With the absence of both furniture and fittings, the sounds of my eagerness were substantially amplified. This unusual timbre caused some strange sounds to reflect back for all to hear. As I continued forward, I was convinced I heard a word or two in the ether. I soon realised that as I progressed further into the house, I was picking up an occasional snippet of conversation between both of my companions, "A bit dreary if you ask me." Joel said in an unusually negative tone. Followed by Mr Glasspool's professional patter, "No, no, no! I would say more cosy, maybe tranquil with a hint of history." Joel added, "It hasn't even got a back door! How are you expected to use just one entrance?" Joel's remarks highlighted a quirk I had not realised, but still I thought the positives far outweighed the small negatives.

I soon left them to it as I went from room to room, imagining how each would look once they had been decorated. *Perfect,* I thought.

The kitchen required a complete makeover, since this seemed to be the room most neglected and may well have been untouched since the 1940s. The floor was of worn stone, especially next to an area of no real significance. This area was next to and between an Aga and a small walk in cupboard, which I guess, had once been used as a larder. I ventured inside and found it empty, save for a mass of cobwebs and an old shallow square box on an upper shelf. At a stretch, I reached up on tiptoe so I could examine the box closer. As I tried to lift the box, I found myself covered in a white powdery residue. This was due to the amount of dust upon it. By disturbing it, I had created a small but distinguishable haze. This miasma soon filled the air causing me to splutter. The box was made of tin, which was overlaid in faded writing and some gilded framed pictures of the Queen's 1953 Coronation celebrations. I shook it gently… it rattled. With a certain amount of excitement and out of curiosity, I opened it to find a solid and heavily blackened key. The stout key had attached to it, a small but brighter chain, which was unlike any I had ever seen before. Each link in the chain was made up of a different design. It went from a plain circular pattern to a diamond, then a star amongst other shapes before finally finishing in a heart shape. I rolled the key around the palm of my hand and watched the blackness of age fall away. Within moments, it had lost its gloom and appeared almost new. With the newness came the warmth. It was at that very moment, I knew without doubt, that I was going to make this my home. I felt the urge to link the chain into a complete circle but screamed, as a heavy hand on my shoulder suddenly curtailed my deep thoughts. Joel screamed too as I spun around and lashed out catching him on the top of his head with the heavy key. He backed away and cowered as if I were a vision of hideousness. I immediately dropped the key and ran to his aid wondering if I had added injury to his earlier bout of misfortune.

With care, I led Joel outside to the front where there was a bench. Here, I inspected the area he was now rubbing vigorously, "Joel, stop that and let me see if there is any damage." I urged.

He lowered his hand and immediately put it back as I prodded the area, "Ouch! That was uncalled for." He bemoaned. I giggled more out of relief at seeing nothing more than a small lump forming on his crown. Joel soon joined in and thumped me reasonably hard on my shoulder, to which I poked his bump again.

Whilst this was going on a disgruntled looking Mr Glasspool joined us and sighed rather loudly, "I suppose I am here under false pretences and you no longer wish to make a bid for Rose Cottage? All this and the car, which would probably need hundreds, if not thousands spent on it to repair. My God, what a waste..."

I stood up and faced him before uncharacteristically placing my hand over his mouth, "Don't despair Mr Glasspool. My mind is more than made up and I wish to make an offer that nobody will be able to meet..." Before adding defiantly, "...And as for your car, I intend to bear the full costs of its repair, providing I win the auction." With that, I pulled out an envelope from my bag and handed it to him. Long before we arrived, I knew what I wanted and had written down a figure I thought would see off any serious competitors.

There was a curious look in Mr Glasspool's eyes as he stumbled over his words, "But..., you see..., I cannot guarantee the outcome of the auction. Besides there is the little matter of..." Once again, I placed my hand over his mouth not wanting him to finish the negative sentence. The man before me was now a shadow of his recent self, and almost relieved that he had received at least one offer for the property following his mornings failed efforts.

I took ten steps back from where Mr Glasspool was standing and looked up at the bedroom windows before stating, "No, this is where I intend to live and nothing is going to get in my way. Now, you two stay here while I go upstairs and finish off the inspection."

The stairs were situated not far from the front door and adjacent to the lounge and kitchen. Almost every step creaked as I jauntily took each one in my stride. The landing led me into three bedrooms, which all appeared airier than the lower floor. I soon found a bathroom that lacked both a bath and more importantly, the room to place one. There was only one fitment in the room, which was a brown stained sink that constantly dripped from the right hand tap. My mind, by now, was moving swiftly, 'Yes.' I thought, 'A shower in here and an ensuite in the larger bedroom. Perhaps knock into the neighbouring bedroom and convert that one into a study.'

The final bedroom would just about take a wardrobe, a single bed and a bedside cabinet. Anything more would just about take the cosiness out of it. Thinking out aloud I said, "Hmmm, perhaps this should be the study…" Before concluding, "We'll see."

With a complete colour scheme in mind, I left the airiness of the upper floor and re-joined my companions. Mr Glasspool was quietly sitting with Joel who was looking quite unwell, although I heartlessly dismissed this, at least temporarily.

I sat between them, and for the first time looked at the distant treeline and beyond. A hazy mauve hillock shimmered in the afternoon heat and bizarrely gave the appearance of nature dancing to a seductive tune being played by Paganini or Tartini. My gaze became transfixed by this quirk of vision and I soon found myself being drawn in by its mesmerising beauty.

My thoughts were suddenly broken as Mr Glasspool rose from the seat. He sighed noisily and proceeded to lock the front door, which then reminded me of the key I had found earlier and had so unfortunately hit Joel with. Before I could ask to retrieve it Joel moaned, "I don't feel so good!"

My assumption that Mr Glasspool would let me have the key was nothing short of ridiculous really, and not a little arrogant. Anyhow, at this point I realised that Joel really needed help.

Chapter 7

Difficult Times Ahead

We said our goodbyes to Mr Glasspool and not before time too, since Joel looked really rough and was still complaining of a headache. Not surprising, as I had just inadvertently bashed him on his head with the heavy key I had found and so eagerly wanted. I had never seen him act so strangely. His manner by now, was giving me more than a casual cause for alarm.

With some difficulty, I eased Joel to the car and managed to strap him into the passenger seat. By the time I had finished with Joel, there was no sign of Mr Glasspool and I had therefore, lost the means of direction back to the main road. Without thinking, I turned left at the end of the lane and did not realise until far too late that I had taken a wrong turn. With Joel looking worse for wear, I started to worry, and soon put behind me any thoughts of the cottage. I eventually found myself on the A354 and therefore unintentionally ended up going away from my intended route. In fact, I was going in the completely opposite direction! Making a rash but fortuitous decision, I headed down the A350. Here, the signs were indicating that I was heading for Poole, where I hoped I would find some form of medical assistance since Joel's needs now looked grave.

By the time we arrived at Poole hospital, I knew that fortune had played its hand, as by now, Joel was unconscious. Screeching to a halt outside the main door, I got out and ran in seeking urgent assistance. Fortunately, I was greeted by a doctor who looked as if she was about to end her shift. The look of concern on my face meant she took my pleas as being serious. The doctor dashed to the door and pressed an emergency button located somewhere out of sight before rushing back to check on Joel. I did not know what my role in all this was so I blindly headed for an inner door as it flew open outward and towards me. Rapidly heading my way, were two quick reacting porters wheeling a stretcher of sorts. For some reason, I ended up in a part of the building well away from where Joel was being tended. Through a window, I could see them place Joel onto the trolley, and it wasn't long before they rushed past me while shouting out stats as one added, "Another one of those druggies I suppose!" In their rush, they had either not seen me or had ignored me as a casual bystander. The doctor looked at me with some sympathy though, knowing that this was not the case, but said nothing as she quickly turned to assist her ill-informed colleagues.

Within seconds, Joel was out of my sight, and for the first time today silence descended upon my life.

I looked around and felt strangely alone. The place was empty save an occasional glimpse or two of people getting on with whatever they were doing. Perhaps it was loneliness, I don't know but my resolve suddenly gave way to desperation as I recalled other times in my life when I felt this much isolation. Although there were more recent times where I felt this desperate, my mind in this situation only seemed to focus on one person… Sarah Littlejohn. In this strange sanitised environment, I felt vulnerable since everything around me seemed big and somehow appeared out of reach. I collapsed to the floor crying out, first Sarah's name then Joel's whilst repeating the word 'sorry'. I seemed to be in a state of despair for ages, but it wasn't long before a stranger helped me to my feet. The unkempt looking man took me to a vacant seat before handing me a set of car keys. He then walked off before I could thank him for showing pity, although he did mutter something as he left, *"You mustn't invite her in!"*

Through teary eyes, I watched his dishevelled form disappear into the distance.

Needing fresh air, I followed the same route the man had taken but was more than surprised that it led no further than into a long dark corridor. The corridor felt extremely cold and looked to have no ending. Already, shaken, I dared not venture any further so decided to go back the way I came and soon found the main entrance and the car.

The cold night air hit me like a hammer and the stinging rain that was now falling brought me back to reality. What had happened to the sunshine and the time, and where was Joel? I was unsure how much time had elapsed since we arrived, but it seemed like an eternity. It wasn't until I felt the car keys in my hand, that I realised Joel's car had been safely parked in a bay opposite. Although the bay in question indicated it was reserved for doctors only, I didn't have the will or inclination to move it. I stood there for a while, with my head stooped, trying to make sense of this whole weekend. By the time I looked up again, the rain had eased. The windscreen of the car reflected the night sky and occasionally revealed the brightness of the moon as the rain filled clouds moved on.

Still feeling uneasy, shaky and slightly cold I headed back inside to see if I could get some answers about Joel's condition. Here I hit a wall of silence, until the doctor who greeted me earlier emerged from a side door. I got up and approached her, "How is he? How is Joel? Is he going to be all right?" These were just three of the many questions I felt I needed answers to.

The doctor led me to a side room and sat me down. She sat too, and in doing so, a strand of her blonde hair fell forward, "Hello…, Miss…, Miss?"

It took me a long time for me to realise that she was actually trying to communicate with me despite the questions I had put forward, "Oh, sorry, yes. You'll need my name… My name is Chambers… Um, Claire…Yes, Claire Chambers. Is he going to be all right?" I asked again.

The doctor studied my face for a second or two before responding, "Hello Claire, I am Doctor Suzy McMillan, part of the Neurology team and I want to reassure you that we are doing everything we can for your friend. Joel, did you say? Would you mind if I asked you a few questions about him?"

"No, I mean yes… that's fine."

"Okay. Are you are relative of Joel's? Or a friend"

I merely nodded.

She frowned, "We need to know which…?"

"Oh, yes, um, a friend. I'm his friend. He has no family, just me."

The doctor smiled and continued, "Okay, thank you. You see, we believe your friend is suffering from concussion or some other related issues, so we have already initiated a CT scan. Do you know if he is on any medication? We also need to know if he has a history of blackouts or other related issues."

I answered all the questions the best I could.

As she left my side, Doctor McMillan reassured me that Joel was in the right place and with the best team the hospital could assign to him. As a parting shot, she shocked me with a snippet of information, "We shall probably induce him into a full coma while we examine all the possibilities. By doing this, we will be protecting the brain while we investigate our options." With that, she vanished, leaving me feeling even more confused and vulnerable. I got up and left the room in the hopes of catching her but she was too quick for me. I watched her as she entered a room and tried to follow, but realised the door was operated by a central electronic key, which automatically locked the door after it closed.

Feeling somewhat helpless, I staggered back to my original seat and sat down whilst mulling over what had just taken place. The only tangible word I actually absorbed from the brief conversation I had just had with Doctor McMillan, was 'Coma'. Then it struck me... Was I was the cause of this when I accidently hit him on the head with the key I had found in the box? Surely not though. I tried to argue with myself that it may have had more to do with his unusual behaviour before leaving London and later, at the Silver Plough. Leading up to this tragedy, I already felt uncomfortable with Joel's extreme and strange behaviour, but shrugged it off. I didn't know any more, as my mind was turning to mush and everything started to blend into one surreal picture.

I tried to relax my mind, and as I did it drifted back through the days' events, and I realised it was finishing in as much a bizarre way as it had started. My obsessive nature of late, had me questioning why I was actually there, and not enjoying a large glass of wine at home. The thoughts centred on the fanatical need I had to own Rose Cottage. Why? I had the money to live anywhere I wanted. I could even afford to live in London's most sought after locations. So why Rose Cottage? My jumbled thoughts had soon become fixated on what some would see as trivia, whereas I should have been concentrating on my dear friend Joel's immediate health. Then, to make matters worse, and like a quick flick of a switch, I selfishly hoped that my sealed bid to Mr Glasspool would be successful. All of a sudden, I had gone from a collective concern for Joel to becoming an individual bathing in self-pity and the desire to own a property I didn't know anything about.

I stood up and shook myself down before walking to the large glass window next to the entrance. The reflection showed an unkempt manifestation of its original self. In other words, it was me - but on one of my really bad days. This sight reminded me of whom I truly was and I decided now was a time for decisive action. I had to take control of the situation.

Despite the size of the hospital, there were so few people about. Even the reception-cum- nurses' station was deserted. But it was by now quite late. Although I didn't have access to all of the doors, I ventured deeper into the building to find someone to talk to about Joel. Finally, I found a doctor who looked at me with suspicion. "Excuse me, Miss. Can I help you?" He asked.

I responded with an air of false authority, "You may indeed. In fact you could do better than that, by escorting me to the Neurological Unit where I believe my friend might be."

His response was as to be expected, "I'm sorry, I cannot do that since I don't know who you are or what you are doing here."

I was ready for that and reached up grabbing him by the collar, "Listen! I have had a fucking long day and I am a teeny-weeny bit pissed off knowing that my friend is in there somewhere and needs me.

Either you take me there or I'll…" I didn't have an 'or I'll' and was trying to think of one when I heard a familiar voice from behind.

"It's okay Stuart, I'll deal with this." I looked around and saw Doctor McMillan, "Claire, I have been looking for you… I need to give you some details of new developments. Would you mind following me?" She led me to another private room where I was politely invited to sit, "We have just got the results of the CT scan we have done for your friend Joel, and it shows that he has a swelling on the brain. It is currently unclear what is causing the swelling but it might be a bleed. The cerebrospinal fluid is being severely restricted by this swelling in the brain, thus causing his current condition. You may well have seen a change in his personality or change of moods recently. Either way, we need to transfer him to Southampton General Hospital where they have a specialised Neurosurgery Unit. This transfer is time-critical and transport has already been arranged... it will be here very soon. Incidentally, we have all had a long day so I suggest you find somewhere to stay and travel to Southampton in the morning. You will not be doing Joel any favours if you end up exhausted and behaving in an unsuitable manner, and believe me; I think you may have just stepped over that mark already!"

I smiled at first as I recalled something Joel had once quoted, 'The brain..., mans' second favourite organ!' and then burst into tears, knowing my initial bravado had come to nought.

Maybe it was my dramatic reaction that made Doctor McMillan take further pity on me. I don't know, but she hugged me and said, "Look, I know this must be a very stressful situation for you, and you must be extremely tired. It's late now, why don't I make a call and try to get you booked in to the nearest Holiday Inn. You can try to get some rest and we can talk again in the morning."

I just nodded, too tired to respond. Doctor McMillan disappeared in the direction of the nurse's station... It wasn't long before she returned.

"Unfortunately there has been a large conference at the Holiday Inn today and they do not have a room, but..." I let out a another sob, before she continued, "I don't live far from here and I have now missed my last bus home, so if you could provide me with a lift, I could put you up. Anyway, I doubt we will find you anywhere else now at this time of night."

I graciously accepted her invitation, greatly touched by her unexpected kindness.

Chapter 8

Voices

The following morning I awoke at eleven and in my confused state, I studied the room I found myself in. A cat was fast asleep at the foot of the bed, which added to the dreamlike sensation I was experiencing. 'Where on earth was I?' I questioned. It came to me in short bursts as I relived the memories of the night before. I suddenly sat bolt upright as I realised where I was and why I was there.

The small box room, just about had enough room to swing a cat. I inadvertently threw the covers off and swung round to sit on the side of the bed, tossing the sleeping cat into the air, which only added to my previous observation about cats. I found the ensuing silence eerie. The cat hissed at me as I was leaving the room then struck out catching me on the ankle. I gave out a little yelp but carried on my way, not realising I was bleeding from a three clawed series of scratches. Initially I looked for the bathroom, and found it at the third attempt. Here, I did my best to make myself look a bit more presentable, knowing I still had a long day ahead of me. Finally, I ventured downstairs and found the kitchen where I was greeted by Doctor McMillan, "Good morning Claire, how did you sleep?"

My reply was more in the form of a question than anything else, "Fine, thank you. Do you have any news?"

A mug of coffee was thrust into my hands, "Too soon to tell I guess, although a colleague of mine did ring to say that Joel had arrived safely and that they are taking good care of him. I'm surprised the phone didn't wake you, although you were pretty out of it last night, you must have been exhausted."

I sat at the kitchen table and unceremoniously placed my mug down, spilling some of the content before running my hands over my face. Without thinking, I then dragged my hands through my hair, "Is he going to die, Doctor?" At last, I finally said what I was thinking.

The doctor joined me at the table, "Please… call me Suzy. I have a good record at reading these situations and I have to say that I am optimistic for your friend Joel, although we must remain extremely cautious. In fact, when you told me that you had accidently hit him on the head, I knew he had been spared a more traumatic event. You see, by hitting him where you did and assuming you had caused him some harm, you did him a favour, as you then sought medical help. Had he continued without your intervention, then who knows what might have happened?"

I had no recollection of telling her about the knock to the head I had inadvertently delivered, but I felt heartened by her response. Somehow though, the words 'extremely cautious' she had used earlier were rather chilling.

Without explanation, I suddenly had an urge to leave but suppressed the feeling, knowing I had my host to thank for many things, including her generous hospitality. Racing to Southampton would not achieve anything, although I felt that was where I should be.

At this moment in time, all thoughts of Rose Cottage had been erased from my mind. However, this was to be short-lived.

Doctor McMillan's kindness would eventually see us become lifetime friends. For now though, I had another long day ahead and plenty of miles between Joel and me.

Before I left, I was instructed again to address Doctor McMillan as Suzy, although this initially felt strange. Suzy made one phone call on my behest to check on Joel's current condition. This, apparently, looked promising although still regarded as 'critical'. Somehow, I had never applied the word critical to Joel's condition before and this struck me much harder than I thought it would, "Critical?" Was all I could say upon hearing such news. Suzy reassured me that in this sense, it meant there was still some way to go but he was in the very best of hands.

I dropped Suzy back at the hospital, before heading for Southampton. It wasn't long before I got lost due to my wandering mind. I pulled over and an elderly couple directed me to the A338, which I was assured, would lead me to the A31 before reaching the M27. The act of asking for directions brought to mind Joel's recent failings on trying to negotiate out of London to find the cottage. This thought caused me to smile at a time I most needed to.

The hospital was vast, and finding the Neurological Unit was harder to find than at the hospital in Poole. Eventually, I found myself being directed to a ward where I spoke to the senior doctor on Joel's case. His best reassurance was that of Suzy's, which was that he was 'in good hands'. I was somewhat alarmed to learn that there was not an operation scheduled for the immediate future.

Apparently, the induced coma was serving well to reduce the swelling. Regardless of this, the doctor thought Joel would still need an operation at a later date. I thanked him for both his help and honesty before asking one more question, "How long will it be before I can see him?"

The response was better than I had hoped.

The doctor looked at his watch before replying, "Oh, I would say that you can see him within the time it takes us to reach the room he is in."

We walked a short distance where I was suddenly hit with the seriousness of Joel's condition. What greeted me was a scene I had hoped I would never see again. Joel was connected to a series of wires, which were attached to a very familiar looking machine. The machine was omitting a regular and not so welcome sound. The beeping of the machine was enough for me to feel desperate about the situation and, once more, my heart sank. It took some time for me to focus on Joel who looked so peaceful. His serene face far different to my heavily furrowed brow. He looked so diminutive and vulnerable that I wanted to cradle him like a baby. It was obvious there was no way I was going to be able to get too close to him, however, but the doctor did advise me that I could hold his hand and speak to him quietly.

I was given ten minutes, although it wasn't long before the senior doctor approached me, "Miss, may I have a word with you please?"

I responded only after he asked for a second time, "Oh sorry, yes of course."

The reason for the consultation was purely to confirm details about Joel's background and to ask for my details just in case they need to contact me. It was the need for my details, and the fact that they would need to contact me that frightened me the most. Why would they need to contact me? Is something going to go wrong? Am I going to be required to authorise the machine to be switched off at some stage? My mind was going in to overdrive merely on the suggestion that they may need to contact *me*. "Why would you need to contact me so urgently?" I asked, confused.

The response was not what I had expected, since I had clearly taken the question to a new and higher level, "I didn't actually say that we would need to contact you urgently. It is just in case we need to speak with you, nothing more than that really. Look, I suggest you go home and I promise you two things. One - I shall personally contact you if there is anything that we have to tell you about his condition. The second point is - if you feel the need to call us at any time then your call will be given priority. I can't say fairer than that now can I?"

I had to agree, and was about to say so, when suddenly I had an idea - perhaps one I should have thought of earlier. "Doctor, can we move him to a private hospital in London so I can be closer to him? I have the means to…"

My question was greeted with a certain amount of disdain, "Look…, your friend Joel has already been moved once. Believe me, it has nothing to do with money since we have, perhaps, the best facilities in the country right here in Southampton. Furthermore, his stability is our overriding concern and it would not be advisable to move him for no other reason than for him to be close to you. Perhaps, may I humbly suggest that if you already have the means, then your money would be better spent on renting a property closer to this hospital."

This response once more shook me into reality. Surely, after what I had already gone through, this was something I could have thought of myself. He was, of course, right.

For the time being though, I returned to the room I had reserved in the hotel. I don't know how much time went by, but I finally got a call that afternoon to tell me that surgery had been scheduled for the following day. I drove straight to the hospital early the following morning. As he went down to surgery, hours were spent pacing the corridors and the grounds of the Southampton General Hospital. How many times I looked at my watch and didn't actually register the time was incalculable. I looked about me as I paced through the grounds, and I swore I saw people moving in slow motion. Small plumes of smoke coming off their cigarettes appeared to just hang in mid-air despite there being a brisk breeze.

Understandably, I was so attuned to Joel's plight that I swore I even heard his voice echo in the breeze. This sound chillingly mimicked the warning I had received earlier from the unkempt man who disappeared after saying the self-same thing, *"You mustn't invite her in!"* Furthermore, I found myself wandering around the cemetery just over the road from the hospital. What was I thinking? In truth, I was not thinking at all, or why I was there – since it was beyond me - and I knew I could do nothing. In Joel's world, the operation, indeed, the whole event would but take a minute… No, a mere nanosecond. However, in my world I had to endure the full horrors of all the possibilities and consequences.

I then had a sudden realisation that I needed to be more positive and busy myself. I left the hospital to think on the future, the present could look after itself for now. Where this realisation came from, I wasn't sure, but lately my reasoning had become much more erratic.

I finally made a clear decision. Earlier discussions had confirmed that Joel would be here a fairly long time. And I had yet to hear about the result of my bid for Rose Cottage. So I set about organising to rent out my London flat. Meantime I found and rented a similarly sized flat near the hospital in Southampton. With a high student population, I had to make do with a property near the 'Common'. This area was bustling with commuters and traffic during the mornings and afternoons but quiet during the evenings.

During this time of 'busying myself', I had regular and extremely positive updates about Joel. Although still in an induced coma, his condition had improved - but had not improved enough for him to move out of the Neuro Intensive Care Unit.

The flat was comfortable and had adequate facilities - although the view across the road was that of a cemetery. Somehow, the link with the cemetery here and the one near the hospital calmed my spirit. There were evenings when I would just sit by the window and stare into the distance. Occasionally, I would take a walk in the peace and tranquillity of the graveyard opposite. Either way, I was just filling in time.

My time at the hospital was limited to certain hours, which although understandable, were far from perfect. While I was with Joel, I would spend my time sitting with him, talking to him and occasionally reading to him.

It was another full month before I finally got a call from Mr Glasspool, "Good morning, Miss Chambers. Providing you can complete a financial transaction by noon this Friday, the property is yours. Although, I must tell you that I am still at odds with the fact that you were the only bidder in this instance. By the way, I also intend to invoice you for the £2,000 it cost me to have my car repaired, which, if I recall correctly, is what you offered to do."

The phone clicked and I thought for a second that I had lost contact before a voice cut in, *"You mustn't invite her in!"* My response was immediate and somewhat discourteous, "What did you say?"

Mr Glasspool sounded pissed off and he responded accordingly, "Now look here. I said I intend to invoice you..."

Instead of having to explain myself I answered in a manner, which appeared just as discourteous, "Yes I got that bit... What did you say after that?"

It was obvious that Mr Glasspool had come to the end of his tether, "Miss Chambers, remember what I said. By noon this coming Friday. Good day!" The phone once again clicked, but I remained on the line for a bit longer. I listened intently, but there was nothing more than an odd crackle or two of static.

I never actually understood why Mr Glasspool held me responsible for the damage to his car, but I did recall the offer I made to cover the costs of repairs, and would of course honour that promise. The money was not an issue from my point of view since I was wealthy enough to absorb the sum quiet easily. For now though, I set that aside knowing my main interest was the successful purchase of Rose Cottage.

It took me a long while before I actually placed the phone back onto the receiver. I felt a shudder go through my body before picking up the phone again and dialling the hospital, "Hello, Neuro Intensive Care please."

It seemed like ages before I was put through to the right department, "Hello, Miss Claire Chambers here, is everything okay with Joel D'Arcy?"

The initial answer was encouraging, "Why yes, he opened his eyes briefly. Please don't take that as a sign of impending improvement, since..." I rudely put the phone down, as the comparison to my Mother's death was too coincidental and in that instance I knew what came next.

I paced up and down before determining what to do.

It was not long before I decided to drive to the hospital and see Joel for myself, and bugger the consequences of arriving out of hours.

There was nobody to challenge me as I made my way to Joel's bedside. Gone were the tubes and his pale face looked tranquil under the stark illumination of the overhead light. "Joel." I whispered. There was a flutter of his eyelids and the faint hint of a smile as he showed signs of recognition. I held his hand gently and in return was rewarded with a firm grasp. I burst into tears.

In this instance, these were tears of joy. And as I later discovered, the news from the doctors was positive. It felt as if huge weight had been lifted from my shoulders and I now knew that everything was going to be all right.

Chapter 9

Moving On

Friday soon arrived, and with funds already transferred into Mr Glasspool's account, I collected a set of keys from a local solicitor's office. These keys excluded the one I had found in the larder and hoped it was still where I had dropped it. With the keys came a pack with specific recommendations and advice on the next steps I should take in the process. The pack suggested several removal firms including that of Cranbury's, which was top of the list. Not having the time to go through all of the options available I decided to give them a ring, "Good afternoon, Cranbury's, how can I help you?" The friendly female voice gave me some encouragement in knowing that I had made the right choice.

My confidence was high since Joel's slow but measured recovery was well underway and I now knew that I could put my all into the move, "Yes, good afternoon." I said cheerfully. "I, um, I don't really know where to start since this is all new to me…" I faltered, although was saved by the positive response.

"Not to worry, we are here to help in any way we can. Perhaps if we start at the beginning and get your details."

From then on, everything was arranged and my role thereafter became lessened knowing I was in safe hands.

For some reason, I deliberately stayed away from Rose Cottage in anticipation of the move. Maybe it was because I felt that that particular day would be a day for me to relish and savour. This was to be an instance in my life, where I just knew everything was going to be right. I also knew that the day of the move was finally going to be that very special day I had always hoped it to be.

The moment eventually arrived and all of my possessions, from both the London flat and my rented accommodation, were loaded into a huge blue and white lorry. I decided to follow the lorry in Joel's car, which I was still using. The lorry driver and his two mates waited patiently, whilst by special request, I made a short detour. This allowed me to call into the hospital to visit Joel.

Joel was now being artificially supported in an upright position, but still not able to communicate properly. Through the edges of the bandaged area on his head, I could see new growth of blonde hair sprouting. For some reason I wanted to run my hands over this small but exposed area of shaven head, but knew I wouldn't be allowed to do so. I could imagine his frustration since he had not fully regained either the power of speech or full upper body movement. However, I have in the past, always gauged what Joel really wanted to express by his eyes. In this instance, he looked serene, although I got the impression that he also wanted to tell me something... something significant. Perhaps my delight in seeing him sitting up and my optimism for the future at Rose Cottage caused me to ignore the latter sign. Whatever it was, it would have to wait. I left feeling more positive than I had in a long, long time.

The moment I had so long looked forward to, had finally arrived.

The build-up to this moment had been tremendous and only compared to my sixth birthday when I anticipated the arrival of a puppy! In that instance what arrived was a complete and utter let down – actually, I had got it wrong - since there was no comparison between a puppy and a what I essentially got which was a walking, talking doll! This time, I knew, there would be no such disappointment.

Everything seemed to be in place and the weather was absolutely perfect for the trip to Pitton. After leading off the main village thoroughfare, we carefully negotiated the narrow and bendy roads. Our arrival at the end of the lane was cut short as the lorry leading the way stopped abruptly. One of the helpers then jumped out of the lorry and ran back towards me. I got out of the car to greet him, "Miss Chambers, we have a slight problem." He turned and pointed, "You see the lorry is too big for us to get all the way down the lane as there appears to be something in the road blocking our way."

My face must have betrayed a twinge of disappointment since everything was going so well up until then, "Oh!" Was all I could offer as a response.

My despair was short lived as I received a positive reply, which once more put a smile back on my face, "Don't worry, we have dealt with worse situations than this. We'll soon sort it out."

I walked up to the lorry and could clearly see the makings of the problem. There was a large pile of earth right in the middle of the road leading up to and towards the cottage. However, and quite surprisingly, it was not too long before a solution was found, as out of nowhere a tractor towing a high-sided flatbed trailer appeared. Because the tractor could not pass the lorry, the two drivers spoke to each other for a while before the removal man approached me once more, "We're in luck! The farmer said he will move the obstruction, but we have to wait while he gets the right equipment. He said something about a snow plough he had."

I looked over to the man driving the tractor and partly recognised him as the same man I had seen herding the sheep on the day of my first visit. Although I saw him, I could not focus on his features as he kept his cap low and his collar up. From what I could see, he appeared to be wearing the same style combat clothing when I had first seen him.

Both the lorry and the tractor moved off road to a site the tractor driver suggested. Here they were able to unhitch the trailer he had coupled to his tractor without blocking the narrow lane. Because of this, I was able to continue as the obstacle was just about the width of half the road. I looked in my rear view mirror to see the trailer-less tractor heading away from the lorry. Without proof, I had a suspicion that the tractor driver had something to do with the pile of earth. I became slightly concerned by this new development. After all, his trailer was empty.

It was not long before I saw 'Rose Cottage' and my heart leapt. Without hesitation, I unloaded a box of essentials, which had been suggested in the pack I received from Cranburys. The suggested items were nothing more than a kettle, tea, coffee, milk and assorted snacks. Within moments, I got to work preparing the kitchen for the arrival of the first 'load'. I was soon fully prepared to welcome the men with a nice hot mug of tea.

Alone in the house, I suddenly found myself feeling uneasy due to a series of rapid tappings coming from above my head. I looked up but could see nothing out of the ordinary and returned to what I was doing. Then something bizarre happened, which made me scream. As if from nowhere, there was a loud crash as the ceiling rose fell and smashed onto the stone floor shattering into what seemed like a thousand pieces. I took three steps back and screamed again as I unwittingly bumped into one of the driver's mates. He too screamed making the whole situation look comical. I laughed nervously and in turn so did he as we both realised how this must have looked to anyone observing the situation.

From where I stood, I looked back at the floor and then the ceiling only to find that there was nothing untoward. There was absolutely no sign of damage or of any debris lying around whatsoever. What had I just experienced? With all the recent activity and upheaval, I put what had happened down as fatigue. Perhaps I had drifted off into a daydream or something. I certainly felt I needed a drink but that would have to wait when things were more relaxed.

The sight of the driver's mate made me realise that the road had finally been cleared. It wasn't long before my furniture and household goods started to appear.

After just under one hour of transfers from the lorry, everything was in situ, which made me realise how little I had. The cottage looked sparse and the sound of emptiness reverberated on occasions as the men brought in the final things from the lorry.

Finally, the courteous driver presented me with a beautiful bunch of flowers. This was soon after I placed the last item to be unpacked onto the small dining room table. Ironically, the last item just happened to be a vase. This coincidental 'finishing touch' made me forget about my earlier scare, which I still put down to tiredness. Before he left, the driver said something quite chilling, "Strange thing about that pile of earth across the road. That farmer chappie who helped us said he had never seen anything like it. Something was said about animal bones. Anyhow, we're off now, enjoy your new home Miss." His comments had me baffled for all of two seconds, as I was bathed in nothing more than the charming surroundings I was now blessed to call home.

Within minutes, silence descended on my world as the last hum of the lorry's engine disappeared.

At last, I was all alone in my own beautiful cottage. As I sat quietly my parents' faces came into my mind, and in a sudden moment of sadness I wished they could be here. Nanny Rose too, but this was a new start and I would have to throw myself into it.

Now that I was alone I could explore and had one specific thing on my mind as I raced to the larder to retrieve the key that seemed so vital to me. There was no sign of the key on the floor where I expected it to be, although the box that contained it was back on the shelf. With extreme eagerness, I reached for it and was amazed to find that it was still covered in dust, almost as if it had never been touched. I shrugged this off and was relieved to hear a rattle coming from within. The lid of the box initially resisted my efforts to remove it, but it soon opened with a resounding 'pop'. With sheer delight I found the key I had for some reason, attached such importance to. As a wave of déjà vu rushed over me, I took it out and once more watched as the dull key turned to an almost new state. This time I took more notice of its transformation before concluding that the heat of my hand was responsible for its remarkable change.

Room by room I searched to find the illusive door that the key would open, only to be disappointed. With reluctance, I placed the key on the bedroom windowsill and in full sight of daylight. Out of the box, the key retained its lustre as the attached chain hung limply, although equally as vivid.

Over the next few weeks I dusted, scrubbed and cleaned until I was satisfied I had everything the way I wanted it. In between bouts of cleaning, I visited Salisbury and ordered some extra furniture, which included a set of dark oak chairs with matching table, dresser and freestanding mirror. I was so pleased with my purchases and gruelling efforts in cleaning, that I sat and stared at my handiwork for hours. It was during this period of reflection that I realised I had neglected everything about my life before I moved in. Hell, I didn't even really know how Joel was. Although the hospital had called with updates, I felt the full weight of guilt knowing how thoughtless I had been. I placed my face in my hands and cried, shuddering occasionally as I gasped in between breaths. What was wrong with me? Why was I being so selfish? These questions kept rising in my mind, especially since Rose Cottage had come into my life. Perhaps I needed to step up and get involved with other things in my life. Actually, there was no 'perhaps' about it as I told myself firmly - *I MUST get out and see Joel - amongst other things.*

I set out the following morning and was surprised to find that Joel had been moved out of the Neuro Intensive Care and onto a ward. I greeted him with a huge smile and was unsurprised when I received a frown back. "Where in fuck's name have you been girl?"

These were the first words I had heard Joel utter since I rushed him to hospital all that time ago. I had no excuses and mumbled an apology, before trying to justify my apparent lack of concern for him, "I've moved in. It's been hard work but the cottage is wonderful." Was all I could add in reply.

In some ways, his behaviour proved to me that he had almost recovered to his normal self. As if to add insult to an already sore wound, I ignored what Joel started to say next as I spied a doctor entering the ward. I approached him much to Joel's disgust, "How is he doctor?"

The doctor looked around a room full of male patients and merely said, "How is who?" I felt foolish as I turned to Joel and merely pointed. Joel slunk down in his bed as the doctor recognised his only patient on the ward, "Oh, Joel. Well I could answer that question if I knew exactly who you are and what connection you have with Mr D'Arcy."

I looked at him with contempt but failed to find a suitable connection to Joel, since I was not a relative, "I, um, well I'm Claire, perhaps he has mentioned me? Um, he is my brother… well practically. Look, we grew up together and I regard him as a brother…"

The doctor raised his hand dismissively and approached Joel's bed with me trailing in his wake. With disregard for my presence the doctor pulled the curtain around the bed, thus excluding me from seeing what was going on. I heard the ensuing conversation, "Hello Joel, how are we today?"

Joel's response was terse and probably aimed at me knowing I could hear everything, even if I couldn't see, "Pissed off!"

The doctor didn't seem to mind the response and continued as if nothing had been said, "Good, good. I have a young lady outside who says she knows you and wants to know how you are."

Once again, Joel responded negatively, "Oh, her, my so-called friend who left me here to rot whilst I was at death's door."

With that, I ripped open the curtain and took two steps forward, "Joel D'Arcy! I know I deserved that but…"

Joel looked at me mischievously, "Oh, hi Claire, how are you? I'm fine by the way - and if you are interested - this is my doctor, who I am hoping will say I can go home soon. Or at least go somewhere where I can be looked after properly when I leave." His point was valid, and well and truly made.

I turned to the doctor and looked for a badge, which would and should have given me his name, "Dr Psycho?!" I exclaimed.

He looked down at his own badge and sighed, "The bastards are at it again." He unceremoniously pulled off his badge and put it in his pocket before adding, "Dr Phillip Szydlo, you see my parents were Polish and the name is a metonymic occupational name for a cobbler…, God! Why am I explaining this to you?" It seemed that he had taken a distinct dislike to me. Before I could protest about it his tone changed, "Look I'm sorry Miss… Claire, I'm having a bad day and I appear to be taking it out on you. Let's step outside for a minute and talk." With that, he pulled the remaining curtain apart and led me away from the sound of Joel having a quiet rant.

As we left, I turned to Joel and poked my tongue out at him.

In light of the name badge debacle, the doctor now insisted I called him Dr Phil, "I'm sorry Claire." He once more apologised and continued, "By his reactions alone I think I have established that you do know Mr D'Arcy." He smiled. "I also know from the way he indirectly spoke of you that you both care for each other, so I'm going to lay it on the line."

I now dreaded the next few sentences, "You see, Mr D'Arcy… Joel that is, has been through a very tough time. In fact, at one point we thought we had lost him. To put it bluntly, he died briefly whilst in theatre. We were able to bring him back. Oh, how stupid of me…, and how obvious is that?" He paused as I tried to absorb what I had just heard. I offered nothing back since I realised I could have lost the only true friend I have ever had, and all I had been thinking about was myself. I looked into Dr Phil's face and could see he realised that I was in some form of shock, "Oh dear!" Was all he could say, as once again as I burst into tears. Not wanting to make matters worse, he was unsure how to react, and sort of patted me on the shoulder and then gave up, which made him look uncomfortable.

This, in turn, made me laugh a little, "I'm sorry." I said.

Dr Phillip Szydlo eventually left me alone, and seemed relieved to do so. Never in a million years had I expected to cope with thought of losing of Joel. I just knew I couldn't live without him, and the news that I might have had to, left me feeling hollow. I chastised myself once more as I re-entered the ward. This time Joel gave me a beaming smile, "Hi Claire, look, I'm sorry. It's this place, it give me the 'Willies' and I can't wait to get out of here. What did he say? Can I go home now?"

I looked at him sympathetically, "I don't know. I didn't ask because… well because." I didn't know what Joel knew so I clammed up and awaited the next obvious question but it didn't come.

There was silence for a while before Joel spoke, "Go on then. Why don't you tell me everything about this cottage of yours then? What is it like?"

It was then that I wondered just how much he remembered so I again asked outright, "Joel, what exactly can you remember since you fell ill?"

He looked at me and frowned, "I'm sorry Claire there is very little I can recall really. I remember arriving at yours and drinking some wine but after that everything is a little bit hazy. Although…" He now looked desperate as his frown lines deepened, "There is something though… Oh, it's no use. The more I try to remember the less I seem to understand. Perhaps in due course everything will come back to me. I don't know."

Joel was looking tired so I made my last comments brief, "You are coming to live with me when you come out aren't you?"

Joel's eyes lit up, "I'm glad you said that. I'm so tired now so you'll have to make the arrangements and just let me know when it is about to happen."

With that, he rolled over onto his left side and sighed.

I left adamant I would make amends by preparing a welcome home surprise for my future houseguest.

Chapter 10

New Discoveries

The preparations went well, and Joel's room was the first to be decorated. It was soon after I had completed this, that I realised I had far too much to do and decided to employ a local painter, decorator and DIY handyman as recommended to me by Stephen from the pub.

Bill was as ancient as the hills, which made me wonder if he was 'up for the job'. We met at the Silver Plough where I was now unexpectedly made to feel like one of the locals. The landlord had laid down several rules with certain members of his clientele. One in particular... I always felt uneasy by way the man with the white beard had looked at me. It was almost as if he had an axe to grind and wanted to bear me ill will. I tried really hard not to make eye contact with him, but I always found this difficult.

Bill was quite amiable and very relaxed, "Bill Evans, Miss." Was his introduction to me before adding, "Stephen 'ere, tells me you might have some work for me." I shook his outstretched giant and gnarled hand, which I found a little bit unpleasant due to its roughness, "Hello Mr Bill Evans, my name is Claire Chambers, but please call me Claire." His wry smile and twinkling eyes soon put me at ease.

After a brief discussion, Bill said he was more than happy with the proposed job, but baulked a little when he found out where I was living. It was almost as if this bit of important information had been deliberately withheld from him. This surprised me on two counts, firstly, why had Stephen not mentioned it to him, and secondly, why this village seemed to thrive on rumour. He cast his eyes around the room as soon as I mentioned the name Rose Cottage. This was followed by a significant silence, which made me somewhat wary since; once again, I felt I was 'missing out' on something that everyone else was privy to.

The white bearded man rose from his seat and took two steps toward the table we were sitting at, before putting on his cap and turning to the door where he left. After that, it took several more drinks for Bill and me to conclude our business… but I was more than pleased with the final outcome. Before Bill and I left, the door opened and in walked a family of three. I guessed they were Father, Mother and their young daughter. They smiled at us as they found an empty table. It was obvious they had been out walking and were keen to take in the pubs delights, atmosphere and warmth. I caught a glimpse of Bill as he smiled gently, such a sweet smile that for some reason I asked him a question, "Do you have children Bill?"

His reply saddened me, "The Missus and me, we had no luck with children. I loved my little girls and we had three over the years. Cot death, that's what they called it then." His eyes filled with tears before adding, "Oh, well, mustn't dwell. Goodbye Miss Chambers, see you soon."

With that, he was gone and I soon followed. I thought about what Bill had just told me, information that perhaps he may not have shared without the courage of a few drinks.

I stopped in the small foyer and gathered a few brochures, which extolled the virtues of local events and places of interest. I wanted to learn more about the area and, hopefully, the people… so I put them in my bag.

When I ventured outside, I saw Bill talking to the man with the white beard. I felt similarly boldened by a couple of drinks and decided to challenge the man. Bill and he parted company, and seconds later

Bill clambered onto his bicycle. Slowly, he wobbled off down the hill to his right, whistling as he went. The bearded man saw me approach and quickly walked away at a remarkable pace. I looked down the hill and saw the tail end of Bill as he disappeared around a corner, the bicycle and he both taking a precarious lurch to the left.

I switched my attention away from the somewhat amusing sight and focused on my main objective. I called after him, "Hello!" I then hurriedly tried to catch up with the mysterious man.

His gait was strange and he walked with his head down and the upper part of his body leaning forward. His style of walking gave the impression that if he were to suddenly stop he would end up top heavy and fall over through lack of balance. I finally caught up with him, but he still didn't stop, so I had to overtake him and stand ahead of him before he would acknowledge my presence. On more than one occasion, he tried to pass me but I stood my ground.

It was only now, that I realised I had to say something and almost lost the power of speech before assertively saying, "Didn't you hear me?"

I then saw a hearing aid and felt a little embarrassed, "Yes, I heard you, I ain't deaf you know! What do you want with me?" He barked.

His aggressive tone narked me so I responded accordingly, "Look, what is wrong with you? You don't know me, so why have you taken such a dislike to me?"

What happened next caught me off guard and scared me as he grabbed me by the arm with remarkable strength. He guided me to a bench next to a bus stop and forced me to sit. What was even more remarkable was his sudden change in attitude as he sat beside me, "Look Miss, I'm sorry. It's not you, you see..., look..., it's that place of yours..., I mean it's my daughter... or rather was... you see, Julianne, my daughter..." He paused a while as if to gather his thoughts, "She used to help out there way back, for Mabel..., you know Miss Adams?", he paused once again, his face etched with pain and discomfort, "One evening she left there and never returned home. We never saw her again. It was as if she... It broke our hearts it did." He put his head in his hands, fighting tears. I hesitantly put my hand on his arm, feeling ashamed of my actions. With difficulty he stammered, "Our l-l-lovely d-d-daughter. G-g-g-one!"

As I was holding on to him, the only thing that came to mind was Sarah Littlejohn. I felt like I was hearing two Father's at once. Both men connected in common grief.

We sat there in silence for some time, both in deep thought. The man then explained that his reaction to me was purely by association with Rose Cottage.

Before we parted, he apologised and turned and introduced himself, "Robin Alsford." He put out his hand and shook mine gently before saying, "I am truly sorry. I'm sure Liz would love to meet you… my wife that is. Perhaps…" He paused once more, and for the first time since I laid eyes on him I saw a flicker of a smile, "…Maybe you could call around one day. It is the small white house just down the lane there on the left." He pointed in the direction he had been walking, "Just call in if you feel the need. You see, we don't have a telephone or any mod cons like that, so feel free to drop in… anytime."

I agreed I would do that. I was glad I had finally found the courage to speak to him.

He stood up and looked down at me, "I am sorry. You know it's just as I said…, I feared you by association. I now regret that. Now that I have met you, I realise what a fool I was for acting that way." He suddenly turned and walked away but this time there was a marked difference in his posture as he wandered off bolt upright. It was almost as if a great weight had been taken from his shoulders. He stopped briefly and shook himself down, as if he too realised the change. I watched him until he disappeared out of sight.

The knowledge I had just gleaned sent a shiver down my spine, as I realised two important things. The first realisation was that there was an association with Rose Cottage and a missing girl. The other, was probably the reason why some of the locals were wary of me. In addition, all this was purely based on the new found relationship to my home. Some of what had been happening had now been explained.

Happily, I put most of what had happened today behind me as I spent the rest of the afternoon finalising some other details. This meant that Joel could rest comfortably in his own room, which I hoped would add to a speedy recuperation. In fact, I was very careful with the layout of his room since I knew his tastes were so fastidious. God he was picky! If anything, I might have gone a little 'overboard' with the feminine charm, since I had deliberately lined up a series of teddy bears along the top of his pillows. I eventually stood back and admired my handiwork, noting a smack of self-satisfaction as I inwardly applauded my homemaking abilities.

I made a final tour of the house and cast a critical eye over everything, noting exactly what I wanted Bill to do. It was through the process of doing this that I looked up at the ceiling in the box room for the first time, it was then that I noticed a small hatchway. Curiosity almost got the better of me as I stared at the well-disguised little hatch cover. In truth, I had no means of getting up there so I added it to my 'to do' list.

In due course, Bill started his handiwork, although he needed some help with the plumbing. He did a remarkable job on both the ensuite and the main bathroom, which both looked pristine when he had finished. In fact, he did remarkably well until he reached the kitchen. Here, he drew the line since the kitchen had not been touched for years, and any refurbishment here was well beyond his skills. Bill suggested a local firm who he had entrusted work to before. I stood back and surveyed the scene before agreeing with him that this particular room needed the most revamping. I asked Bill to make the call, which he was glad to do. Inconveniently, due to their heavy schedule he had to book them for two months hence, so I had to continue to make-do with my dated kitchen for now.

In between getting ready for Joel's arrival and waiting to have the kitchen done, I decided I would concentrate on the back garden. The front of the house was well kept, but the rear appeared rather overgrown. It was at this stage I realised that not having a back door was slightly inhibitive but not insurmountable. Joel was right about the problem with access, but I was not overly worried about this and carried on with my master plan.

This was the very first time I had ventured deep into the garden and was pleasantly surprised by its content. Despite being overgrown, the garden had previously been well managed and seemed to contain a well-selected variety of plants and shrubs. I would deem these as old-fashioned, and Nanny Rose would have easily recognised the plants. This brought her to mind as I tended them. I found Dianthus, Lavender, Boxwood, Jasmine, Forget-me-Nots, Lily of the Valley, Flowering Quince, Phlox, Wild Dog Rose and Wisteria, to name a few. The knowledge I held of florae was down to Nanny Rose's love, which over the years she had passed on to me with relish.

Halfway down the garden was another surprise... I found a simple bridge across a fast running stream. The broad, studded bridge was sound and sturdy, and led to the second part of the garden. Here, I was in a small meadow that led toward the copse at the back. In this section of the garden, I found Red Flax, Cornflower, Painted Daisy, Red Orache, Bishop's Flower, Baby's Breath, Cosmoc with Cornflower, Larkspur and Purple Tansy. There was, however a separate oblong strip of bright red Poppies. This particular area seemed more cultivated than the rest of the garden. Just beyond this point was a remarkably well preserved bench, which I sought out and tried for sturdiness. Here, I felt at home and soon drifted off with thoughts of my future at the cottage... *my cottage!*

I was unsure whether it was the relaxed atmosphere or the headiness of the scented air, but I soon realised I had lost time and found myself in the half-light of the evening. Getting up off the bench proved extremely difficult and I soon found myself struggling to gain enough strength to stand. Once up, I retreated toward the bridge and steadily made my way to the front of the house.

Again, I found the spectacle of the evening sky with its different hues of greys, yellows, mauves and reds spellbinding. It was only now, as I approached the front door and raised my hand to open it that I found the necklace. In my semi-clenched fist, I unexpectantly found a beautiful silver necklace with an angel pendant hanging from its delicate links. I had no recollection of picking it up, or understood how it got there. In fact, looking at my hands I could not explain the traces of dirt, both on and under my fingernails. Despite my good intentions of actually doing some gardening, I never did. The necklace itself was obviously old and was speckled with dirt. On closer inspection, I found the details of the angels face perfectly preserved and remarkably clean by comparison to the chain. As I was studying the necklace I was shocked into reality by the sharp musical ring tone of my phone.

Joel was, by now, his usual self-confident self, "Hi Claire. Are you coming to get me? Everything is packed and I'm raring to go. Come on girl, hurry up."

This caught me somewhat off guard as I was told that he wouldn't be able to 'come home' until he had completed a series of tests, "Joel, are you sure you are alright to come home? I mean…"

Joel stopped me from talking and interrupted with an air of impatience, "Of course I'm all right to leave! I've done all the tests and they want the bed, so come on. Come and get me now!" He screamed the latter part of his sentence, with more than a hint of urgency.

I placed the necklace carefully in my pocket and headed for the kitchen where I washed my hands and collected my keys.

Within two hours, we arrived… not at home but back at the Silver Plough. I was, as usual these days, greeted with a smile and shown to a table in a different section of the pub. I had not been in this part of the building before and it surprised me how big the pub actually was. Stephen explained that they were awaiting the arrival of a group of people who had especially booked the upper section of the pub. As we were seated, Stephen addressed Joel, "How are you feeling now? We were sorry to hear that you felt unwell since your last visit."

Joel looked at me, then Stephen quizzically, "Sorry but I don't recall ever being here before." Curiously, he then looked at me again before asking, "Have I?"

I merely nodded and looked up at Stephen, "Sorry, he does not have much recollection of our visit here." I made a circular sign with my index finger, whilst pointing to the right side of my head.

Stephen laughed quietly not knowing what to make of my little gesture, although a sharp punch on my left shoulder from Joel was accompanied by the words "Oi you! I'm not bonkers you know." We both giggled as Stephen went off to fetch our drinks order.

As Joel laughed, I couldn't help but notice the scar peeking through his new hairstyle. The sight saddened me, especially since I had shown scant regard for his wellbeing over the recent few months. Lately, my thoughts had centred solely on Rose Cottage and there was nothing… or nobody… that could shake this.

It was great to have Joel back, although it wasn't long before I pushed some sensitive 'buttons'. Probing, I once again asked, "Joel, what exactly do you remember now?"

He looked at me and his mood became sombre, "As I said before, I can't remember anything." He grimaced before adding, "Goddamit, why can't I remember?"

The frustration he felt was obvious, so I filled in some of the gaps in the hopes he would recall something. It was after our drinks had arrived that he grabbed my arm and said something strange, "Hang on, I remember two things. One was to do with sheep and their strange eyes…, and, um, and… Oh, bugger, I've lost it. It was something to do with…, hang on I'll get it soon. No, it's gone." Once again, he forcefully said, "Goddamit!" He then placed his hand to his head.

I knew we had reached a point where it would be better to drop the subject, "Don't worry Joel, it'll all come back with time." I avoided the subject for the rest of the evening and was pleased to see and hear that the old Joel was back…, or, at least, mostly back.

We arrived home late that night by taxi. Joel was suitably impressed with his room and particularly with the row of teddies. The grin on his face said it all, but I guess some of his glee was down to the amount of alcohol he had recently consumed.

Chapter 11

London Calling

Over the ensuing month or so, Joel gained his momentum. He had gathered enough strength to be involved with housework and other menial tasks. This particular Tuesday proved to be special since he decided he would take me out for lunch.

We travelled into Salisbury by taxi and found a cosy pub in the centre. Joel was now beginning to feel more comfortable about talking openly about his illness. Often, there were moments when he would clam up, especially when I mentioned the sheep once more. I soon learned to avoid this subject, even to the point of not ordering the 'dish of the day' - lamb shanks. We also agreed not to broach the subject again unless it was on Joel's terms, which probably meant never! The foremost point of this discussion though, was to see if he could recall the second thing that he wanted to tell me when he came out of hospital. Once again though after several discussions we drew a blank.

The ride back to the cottage proved a great source of amusement to us both as, more than a little bit tiddly, we giggled at almost everything the other had to say. The taxi dropped us off and the driver appeared more than keen to leave and return to the city.

The freshly finished decorating had changed the ambiance of the interior, and the new furniture lessened the echo that had plagued the house from the start. Piled in one corner of the kitchen was a selection of Bill's tools and equipment. These were alongside some of the new cupboards that awaited the fitters. This was the only room to have some form of wallpaper, which was dull and dreary. Stripping off the ancient wallpaper meant all that was required to finish the off the decorating was the removal of the old fittings and the installation of the new. Bill could then finalise it all with a 'lick' of paint.

Mischievously, Joel pointed to the stepladder in the furthest corner before sniggering and slurred, "Hey Claire, what do you say to us opening that loft hatch?"

Without thought of our current inebriated state, I readily agreed. We grappled with the ladder before making our way up the stairs, which must have looked hilarious from any angle. We had managed to get the ladder under the hatch but struggled to position it in the right place. Joel clambered up the ladder as it creaked perilously under his weight. I vaguely remember telling him to be careful amid fits of giggles.

Unsteadily, he reached the top as I fought to control the sway of the ladder but it became too much and Joel crashed to the ground heavily. Unexpectedly he burst out laughing, almost uncontrollably, which caused me to join in whilst also trying to ask if he was okay. Had I been sober, I would have been more concerned for Joel than I currently was, but alcohol tempered my overall concern. He stood up and tried once more although he needn't have bothered, since no matter how hard he tried he could not budge the cover. I ducked more in theatrics than anything else, as he wobbled once more, "Bugger, it won't shift."

We soon gave up and went downstairs to polish off whatever we could find in the way of alcohol.

I awoke with a pounding headache punctuated by a loud tuneful noise. It took time, but I soon realised it was my phone again, "Uh, hello." Was all I could offer the pleasant sounding voice on the other end.

"Good morning Miss Chambers, I am Claudia from Mr Adrian Newry's office."

"Morning?" I queried before questioning the name and the nature of the call without too much style, "Who? What?"

There was no getting away from the politeness of the caller, "Claudia… Mr Newry, your parents' solicitor in London."

From the fuzziness of my hangover I suddenly recalled the name, "Oh, *that* Mr Newry! Sorry, how can I help?"

The response was precise, "We need you to call into the office to sign some documents. It has something to do with the transfer of money from one account to another. There is no possible way we could rely on the post, also the document needs witnessing. So, if you could offer a date and time, then perhaps we can see if we could fit you in."

As far as I was concerned, a trip to London at any time would be an inconvenience. It didn't take too long for me to respond, "Uh, well today is…" I paused thoughtfully, "…Tuesday, no Wednesday." Without too much deliberation and in frustration, I came up with a rather strange suggestion, "Um, how about later this week? Shall we say Friday? Noon maybe?"

At no time did I even question why there was a need for the money transfer since I knew that would be explained in due course.

There was a brief pause from the other end, "That would be fine but could you make it 1:30?" I thought for a while and concluded that the suggested time would be better as I suddenly realised the distance involved. I agreed the time. "Thank you Miss Chambers, we look forward to your arrival."

Wearily, I placed the phone on the floor where I had just woken. I then turned to see Joel lying at an acute angle on the other side of the room. Mischievously, I got up, walked over to him and tittered as I poked him into awareness. He blinked, rubbed his eyes and focused on me, "Hey girl!" Was all he could say before trying to stretch and yelped as he did so, "Ouch, what the fuck did we do last night? I'm as stiff as a board and my shoulder hurts like hell."

For once, I was none the wiser since I too struggled to remember what we had been doing. Joel got up painfully and staggered to the kitchen to make coffee. I soon joined him and slowly, but surely it dawned on me what had happened. The reason for this revelation was the array of items belonging to Bill being strewn all over the floor, coupled with the absence of his stepladder. Whilst Joel prepared the coffee, I ventured up the stairs noting that there were several chunks out of the wall and various scratches to the new paintwork. I cringed.

Not wanting to venture any further, I returned to the kitchen in silence and readily drank two cups of coffee before speaking, "Joel, I know what we did last night."

Joel looked more shocked than curious, "Oh God, what did we do? Please don't say anything tacky happened!"

I pointed to the mess behind him but this didn't seem to stir any memories, so I told him. "Oh, thank goodness for that. You had me worried there for a minute." For now, nothing more was mentioned about the nights' frolics but it did play on my mind.

Joel finished his coffee and declared that he needed to get some 'proper' sleep and politely said 'night' before heading for the bedroom. I, on the other hand, felt the caffeine hit and was soon wide-awake.

After washing up and clearing away the general untidiness I decide to carefully remove the ladder and replace it to its original home. However, once at the bottom of the ladder, I felt compelled to climb it to see if Joel's half-assed efforts had loosened the hatch. To my utmost surprise, I felt the hatch move with ease and almost fell off the ladder as I had put a certain amount of effort into the push. With caution,

I poked my head into the gloom and almost screamed as I felt something touch my head. With a quick flick of my hand I tried to brush away, what I was certain was a spider's web. The so-called 'web' turned out to be a cord attached to a small ceiling rose. This, in turn, when pulled switched on a centrally fitted light. The light flickered several times, which was just enough for me to see that the loft was not empty. Before I could see anymore, the light brightened and went bang with a sharp pitch. Deciding better of the situation, I lowered the hatch and sought out the safety of the floor.

I returned to the kitchen and made myself another coffee. As I stood next to the new flat pack cupboards, I spied a large rubber torch in one of Bill's boxes. It was too tempting for me to ignore since curiosity had, by now, grabbed me and led me to my next course of action. The torch was heavy and very powerful, which was exactly what I needed as I headed back to the small box room where the ladder stood.

Without caution, I climbed the ladder and threw open the hatch before switching on the torch, which flooded the gloom with light. Now, I could see what only a moment earlier, was a fleeting glimpse. There were a few packing cases, a small table, two chairs and something bulky under what looked like a floral blanket. The dusty floor was lined with panels and looked robust enough for me to walk on so I ventured in, carefully testing my footing as I went. The cobweb lined roof beams looked sturdy and some appeared almost new, although this might not be the case so I remained cautious. There was no lining to hide the beautifully laid out thatch, which appeared intricately woven and tied off. Then there was the smell. I wouldn't say it was musty but it had the smell of age and bore the dry aroma of hay. I remembered this smell from my childhood and recalled rolling in the haystacks when out in the country.

Up here, I felt comfortable until I heard a sound coming from behind. In fear of rats, I flashed the torch around quickly but couldn't see anything and backed away from the source of the noise in anticipation. My progress backwards was stopped when my leg meet something solid. I hastily spun around. At first, I couldn't see anything until I lowered the beam onto the bulked up floral blanket I had seen earlier. My heart leapt in eagerness as I slowly pulled back the blanket and was stunned by what I saw. I had revealed a perfect replica of Rose Cottage. Excitedly, I threw the dusty blanket to one side to expose its full glory. The flawless features of the cottage had been gloriously captured in miniature. I glanced around it but was disturbed by another sound from behind. Once again, I flashed the powerful beam around the room and could see nothing other than a stream of natural light pouring in through the opened loft entrance. Until then, I had not realised I had ventured so far into the room. I suddenly became aware of the distance just before I saw some movement in the top right hand corner of the thatch. The beam of light from the torch found its target as I heard a squeal of discomfort and saw some agitated movement. Four bats suddenly flapped their wings as if to shake off the light - and they were successful as I lowered the beam and bolted for the hatch.

Had it not been for Joel responding to the noises I had been making, I could have had an accident as I missed my footing on the ladder. He quickly assessed the situation and grabbed the base of the ladder, which brought to an end the wobble I had caused in my haste. I fell into his arms and laughed more out of relief than anything else, whilst brushing something invisible out of my hair.

Joel looked startled, "Are you alright? I heard a scream and all hell seemed to break loose above my head."

I looked at him in a startled sort of way before thanking him for his heroism. Joel thought enough was enough and folded the ladder before placing it back to where it belonged in the kitchen. On the way, he managed to gouge out more sections of the wall. "Oh, well!" I muttered to myself.

When Bill arrived, I had to apologise about the gouges in the stairwell wall before explaining what I had found. I asked him if he could go up into the loft and see if he could change the bulb. I quickly explained that I was sure it had merely burned out. He declined and said he wouldn't touch the electrics but would call a 'mate' who would look at it. I, somehow, got the impression he was more reluctant to enter the loft room for reasons other than he had suggested. Perhaps my mind was working overtime but I swore I saw him shudder when I mentioned the loft.

Later that day, the kitchen fitters arrived and were keen to get on, although they soon found a reason not to install the cupboards since they needed the walls to be stripped of wallpaper. They also found certain elements were missing from some of the essential fittings and needed to get them. It was mutually suggested that they came back at a later date. This somehow didn't seem to bother me since I proposed they came back on the Monday after my London visit. By then Bill would have stripped the wallpaper and partly decorated the walls. With this in mind, I asked Joel how he felt about a long weekend in London, rather than a flying visit. He readily agreed and came up with an array of ideas that would occupy our time there.

Chapter 12

The Call

Friday soon came and at my behest, I suggested to Joel that when we got there, he accompany me into Mr Newry's office so he could bear witness to my signature. Joel was more than eager to head back to London and said, "Fine..., let's get going, we're wasting time!"

However, before we could leave the cottage, I had a phone call from Ida, Bill's wife, "Sorry Miss Chambers but Bill has come down with something. It happens to him sometimes. He is very sorry but will not be around this weekend to finish off the decorating."

I felt disappointed, knowing what this meant. The need to have everything at Rose Cottage finished, seemed more important to me than the trip to London. However, before I could get agitated about the news she added, "Oh, don't you worry though, he has asked his nephew Rodney to do the work for him. He used to be Bill's apprentice you know, so everything will be in good hands. As I said these things happen."

There was a pregnant pause as I drifted off a bit because my mind suddenly wandered to other relevant factors. Joel added pressure by pointing to his watch and mouthed something I couldn't understand. I finally spoke, "Oh, all right, thank you for letting me know. Bye." Whether the conversation was finished from Ida's point of view, I was uncertain as I hung up before she could respond.

Today was also the first time Joel had taken control of the wheel of his car since his 'episode' as he liked to call it. Nervously he sat in the driver's seat and went through something I had not seen him do before. He talked his way through the starting procedure as if to convince himself that he could do it, "Right then. Neutral, Mirror. Claire, how on earth do you see anything in this mirror? It is so low. Right! Where was I? Okay, here we go." The engine burst into life as soon as he turned the ignition key. "Now, which one is the brake?"

I started to explain to him when I caught a glimpse of his wry smile, "Ha, ha, very funny." I said as he laughed at my response.

The trip to London was reasonably uneventful, with the exception of Joel having another laugh at my expense as he feigned a fainting attack on the M3. He had almost convinced me he was having a seizure but couldn't restrain himself as he once more burst out laughing, "Oh, you should have seen the look on your face."

I punched him in the arm. I quite honestly feared the potential threat of him lapsing into a coma or something similar. "Pig!" Was all I could add.

We eventually parked in an underground car park in Park Lane and walked across the road to Upper Grosvenor Street where Mr Newry's offices were. Although half an hour early, Claudia greeted us warmly and showed us through to a waiting room.

Generally, Joel would not really notice women's general shapes, least of all comment on them, but he felt the need to say something when we were alone, "I've worked it out." He said knowing I would respond.

"Worked what out?"

He leaned in closer, "He wants you to transfer the money into an offshore account so he can run away with her. You see, they are having an affair and they have hatched up a plan to elope with all of your cash."

When we finally met with Mr Newry, Joel had a fit of giggles, which was rather off putting... although looking at Mr Newry I understood why he did. You see, Mr Newry was not an attractive man and his twenty-odd stone frame was supported, just about, by bowed legs that a pig could run through. Claudia, on the other hand, was stunningly attractive with great curves, which unsubtly suggested 'Playboy Bunny'. To top this off Mr Newry's chair emitted embarrassing noises every time he moved.

I could feel Joel's tension and asked if we could be excused for a while, then left the room where we couldn't restrain ourselves any longer. With tears streaming down our cheeks it took more than 'the while', I had suggested it would take to calm down. Eventually we were fully composed and returned to Mr Newry's office full of apologies, although I knew Joel was still slightly on the edge. Mr Newry was the ever-consummate gentleman and fully explained why money needed to be transferred and where it was to be transferred. He even went on to explain that I was gaining several thousand pounds in interest on a monthly basis. Once more, I could feel Joel rocking as he was either thinking back to what had just happened or had moved on by twisting yet another innocuous word or sentence. With this in mind I hurried on proceedings and suggested we sign the documents so, 'we could all get on'.

Once outside of the office I asked Joel what else he found so funny and even when he explained I could not understand where he was coming from, "Well, when he said, 'gaining several thousand pounds' and I thought..., Oh, never mind, the moment has gone now. Hey girl, I'm starving, can we eat." I agreed. Anything to get Joel away from this area.

We settled down for a late lunch in a restaurant just off South Audley Street. It wasn't much longer after that, that I had a telephone call from Rodney, "Hello Miss Claire. I'm Rodney and my Uncle Bill told me to ring you if I had a problem." Immediately, I conjured up a series of 'problems' and tried to find an answer for them all, although the one I was about to be given certainly wasn't on the list. He continued, "Well, it's like this you see, I have found a door. Well, I haven't really. Um, what I'm trying to say is that when I took the wallpaper off I found what used to be a door. It's sort of boarded up if you see what I mean."

There was silence for a while as I tried to fathom out where in the room he was talking about, so I asked, "Rodney, exactly where is this door and where would it lead?"

I heard a click on the line and thought I had been disconnected before he came back, "Well you see, it is at the far end of the kitchen next to the larder. It leads into the back garden. The wallpaper is quite old and thick so I'm guessing it has been..." He paused for a while, "...What do you want me to do?"

I told him I would call him back soon with an answer. Joel was as intrigued as I was about this sudden development. We discussed the matter for a while before Joel asked a pertinent question, "How does it fit in with the new kitchen layout?"

I thought long and hard whilst trying to visualise the floor plan that had been taped to the kitchen wall, "I think the space he is talking about is at the end. You know, between the larder and the Aga. If it is, then the door is where the kitchen table was going to be placed." Without realising it, I had already made up my mind by using the words 'was going to be placed'.

I was about to call Rodney when Joel stopped me, "Hang on! What have you decided to do?"

It was rather remiss of me not to include Joel's further thoughts as I added, "Oh, I think it would be a good idea to open it out so I can get to the garden more easily."

Joel agreed in principle but wisely added, "What is involved in opening it up? How much will that cost? And..., and..., Oh, I'm sure there are other things to consider before you decide." I smiled at his concerns and he had raised a good point or two.

As usual, the money was no problem at all but I had not considered the structural side of things, which prompted me to call Rodney back, "Hello Rodney, it's me Claire."

He sweetly relied, "Oh, hello Claire. What shall I do? I don't know what to do… shall I call my Uncle Bill?"

I reassured him that he was not to worry, but asked him to carry on stripping the paper and to decorate as he had originally planned. There was an audible sigh of relief from him as he could now focus on what, I assumed, he did best. Finally, I asked him to give me a call on Monday when the kitchen fitters arrived.

Joel and I were enjoying our fabulous break and lounged around some of our favourite sites. We even booked into the Dorchester where I knew Joel liked to play mind games with the staff. I remember on one occasion when we stayed at another hotel, after a wedding we had attended locally. Here, Joel caused havoc by expertly posing as a Hotel Inspector. He was eagerly taken around the various rooms to prove their worthiness. He pretended to cast a critical eye on absolutely everything and told them a report would be in the post, although for some reason he felt the need to mention a possible downgrading. Obviously, nothing happened, although we were eventually found out and banned for life by the management when they discovered his fraudulent cover. With the situation as it was, I wondered if the ban still applied and on a whim, Joel and I decided to visit the hotel. There was nobody there to recognise us and there certainly wasn't a 'wanted' poster nailed to the wall, so in some ways, we were pretty disappointed.

On the Saturday, I even paid my old office a visit and caught up with the gossip, whilst imagining what it would still be like to be sitting at my workstation. The Saturday shift was a real pain in the arse, but we all had to 'do our bit'... although this didn't seem to apply to the managers. I casually looked around and noted that nothing had actually changed. Sitting at my old desk, I noted the personalisation of its new occupant. There, smiling back at me was a photograph of a handsome young man dressed in skiwear and wearing a multi-coloured bobble hat. It was then that I thought back to the days when I worked here, knowing that Nanny Rose was waiting for me at home. There was some sadness in this thought, but it made me think about the day, not many months ago, when the other 'Rose' had mysteriously come into my life.

Somehow, this spur of the moment visit made me realise just how important Rose Cottage had become to me.

Chapter 13

The Dream

On Sunday night, whilst still away, I had rather a strange dream. It centred on events I had already lived through, as opposed to my normal dream pattern. Normally my dreams seemed to centre on chaos. This dream was different though and was almost like a video in slow motion replay. Firstly, there was the key I found and the events that ensued. In this segment of the dream, I looked at the key with intent. I could feel it in my hands and even recalled the pattern of the 'notched' end. My dream then took me back to the incident in the loft room, although this time some of the things happened in reverse. In this instance, I walked forwards and toward the beautiful doll's house sized replica of Rose Cottage. By now, everything was in slow motion, and because of this, I noticed far more features than I had before. With an unparalleled attention to detail, I noticed the one thing I hadn't before. This particular vivid detail centred on the presence of a backdoor. It was in situ and instantaneously recognised by me as one I had seen before. No matter how hard I tried, I struggled to understand where I had seen it before. I knew I had seen it sometime recently, but its relevance failed to immediately register with me. Then suddenly, in my dream, I heard, in my own voice, the startling words, "Got it... Of course!" This 'eureka' moment came about because I recognised it as the bridge spanning the stream in the back garden. It was, of course, the self-same design as the studded door I was now looking at. Then the dream suddenly took me on another course, where I was just standing in a void.

At this point, I found myself studying the angel necklace I had somehow unearthed on the day I explored the back garden. It wasn't until then, that I remembered I even had it and woke up trying to put my hands in my pocket to retrieve it. Only then, in mid-fumble, did I realise I had been dreaming and even then I had a hard time coming to terms with such a vivid dream. My body was wet with sweat, so I got up and took a shower not knowing or caring about the time. The shower felt wonderful and the cascading rhythm of the water on my head helped me relax. As the water was going down the drain, I remembered I had left the necklace in my jeans pocket, and swore at myself when I realised I had not checked the pockets before I put the jeans in the wash.

It was a good three hours since I had the dream and when I met Joel for breakfast, I was eager to tell him. We chatted together but, impatiently, I felt my conversation was more important than his, so I continued regardless, "Joel, listen to me…" He tried to interrupt again but I gave him no room to speak, "No…, you listen. I had a dream…" Characteristically, he relaxed and settled back in his chair with a fixed grin on his face as I continued, "…about the key, the bridge and the necklace. Oh, I didn't tell you about the bridge or the necklace did I? No? Well I found this necklace in my hand and I didn't know how it got there. I crossed the wooden studded bridge, which took me… you see, the bridge was in the garden at Rose Cottage… but, anyhow, in the dream…" I was now rambling and the substance of the dream suddenly began to fade.

Joel smiled confidently, "I know. The bridge is in the back garden but it isn't a bridge at all, is it?" I stared at him in disbelief as I silently nodded. He carried on, "No, it is the back door isn't it?" Once again, I nodded as he cockily punched the air before adding, "That's it, that's all I've got."

Even this snippet was remarkable enough, so I asked him how he knew. His response was as simple as it could have been, "I dreamt it last night." It was as if he had just won a tournament and with self-satisfaction, he stretched his arms upwards then outwards, leaned back before clasping his hands together behind his neck.

I had plenty of questions, "What do you make of it? I mean, does it mean anything to you? Is it a sign that I should do something about the door?"

Joel continued smiling, "Whoa girl, one thing at a time. Yes, I do think it is a sign. I think it is a sign you should open up the doorway." We awaited the expected telephone call from Rodney.

An hour later, my phone rang. I answered it within seconds, "Hello." I said eagerly.

"Hello Miss Claire, I have the man here who is fitting the kitchen. Here he is… Hang on a minute I'll… Oh, his name is…"

Rodney's voice was quickly replaced by another, as I pictured an impatient man snatching the phone from him, "Hello, this is Noah the kitchen fitter. We appear to have a slight problem and need your input. The way I see it, is that a doorway had at some time been sealed off and papered over. It wouldn't interfere with our work should the entrance be reopened but it would reduce the size of the space you had allocated for the table." Noah had just confirmed my earlier suspicions about the location. He continued, "My chaps are willing to take on the carpentry side of things, although the door might be a problem…"

This is where I cut in, "Hi Noah, I think I might have a solution to the door problem. I might be wrong though." The reason I added the latter, was because Joel had just flashed a written note before my eyes. I continued, "There is a stream in the back garden, which has a bridge over it. The bridge, I suspect, is the door that was once located in the kitchen. Without getting my hopes up, I have been cautioned by my friend here, to say that given the time it must have been out there it might be rotten. I must say though, it felt pretty solid to me. Can you have a look at it and get back to me?"

Noah sounded positive and said he would call back after he had investigated.

Nervously, I waited for the second call and paced up and down. Joel told me that I was now being silly since it was only a door. A door, he added, that could probably be bought from the local DIY store for a few pounds. Somehow, though, this felt as important to me as anything I had recently lived through.

The anxiety I was experiencing went far beyond any normal reasoning. Eventually, the phone rang and I almost jumped out of my skin, "Hello, hello. Noah is that you?"

The phone crackled and a familiar voice answered, "No it's not Noah, it's me Rodney. Do you want to speak to Noah? I'll get him from the back garden if you want."

For some unknown reason I swore before immediately apologising, "For fuck's sake! Look, I'm sorry Rodney. What is it that you wanted?"

He sounded crestfallen, "Oh, I have a message for you from Noah. He said to tell you that the door is in perfect condition but a new problem has come up."

He paused and I felt my blood pressure rising, "And that problem would be what Rodney?" I said through gritted teeth.

He answered meekly, "Oh, it has something to do with the lock… I think."

After a moment's consideration on my part I carefully instructed Rodney to go to the spare bedroom and to look on the window ledge where he would find a key before adding, "Take that to Noah, and ask him to try it."

Despite the fact I said I would hang on, there was a click and the line went dead. Several minutes went by and more frustration built up inside me. Never before had I experienced such apprehension. I am ashamed to say that even the trip from Canada to New York didn't feel as stressful as this. I wondered what on earth was wrong with me.

At last, the phone rang and thankfully, this time it was Noah. "Hello Noah here. I have some good news for you. Remarkably, the key Rodney gave me fitted, and believe it or not, the door is in perfect condition. Almost like new in fact. I don't understand how it remained so well preserved, given the length of time it must have been there. Especially since it was so close to running water. Even the lock shows no sign of rust. We'll fit it tomorrow after we have fitted the kitchen units. By the way, I've already got one of my guys opening the area up and another making the frame."

Although I had not negotiated a price for the work, I could have cared less. All I wanted was for the door to be fitted and in place, by the time I got home.

I thanked Noah and turned to see Joel staring at me, "Wow, when you get a bee in your bonnet you really go for it, don't you? Poor Rodney."

I felt a little foolish knowing how I had just behaved but this seemed so very, very important to me. I then analysed my actions before coming to one conclusion, which I then shared with Joel, "I think I know what it is that is so important. The house is not yet complete. Yes, that is it. Until that door is fitted the house remains incomplete."

Expecting some form of rebuff, I was surprised by Joel's response, "Hey girl, I think you are right."

The rest of our time in London went painfully slowly, and despite enjoying the city, I yearned to get back home.

Chapter 14

Homecoming

I suggested I drive on the return leg but Joel, quite rightly, thought it would be safer if he drove due to my current state of mind. The trip seemed to take an age, even though Joel drove well above the speed limit knowing I was keen to get home. As we sped down the motorway, I continued to wish the miles away.

Closer to home, we were overtaken by an ambulance heading our way. This distraction stayed ahead of us for the last mile or so, yet I watched in horror as it took the turn to our lane and headed toward the cottage. Another emergency service vehicle, in the form of a Volvo car bearing the words 'Paramedic', was already parked on the drive.

Without waiting for the car to fully stop, I leapt out and rushed in to find two casualties being attended to by the paramedics. The first was being treated for what looked like a serious hand wound, as blood dripped down his upright hand and onto the floor. He looked up at me as I entered the room, "Oh, hello Miss Claire, the door's on." This could be none other than Rodney. How he knew who I was, was a mystery but I guess he used what little reason he had to work it out. The second patient was a man who looked in a very bad way. Here, a doctor who must have arrived with the paramedic, was working with the two ambulance crewmembers to treat, as I was later told, an 'acute Myocardial infarction', or heart attack. I was later told that the workmen had encountered a few problems when fitting the door, which I'm guessing, was why they were there today... well beyond the time schedule I was given. They were there since they didn't want to let me down, and had called in early to finish the job. I also found out that the man being treated on the floor in my kitchen was none other than Noah. Apparently, Noah thought all that was needed was one other person to finish the job with him. Rodney offered his services, which meant Noah could release his other men to finish off another job. I was not entirely aware of what happened on that day but concluded something of significance had occurred soon after they fitted the door.

In the meanwhile, my attention was diverted to the presence of the door. It was magnificent! Solid oak, blackened with time… but it didn't take me long to realise there was something wrong. Unbelievably, I skirted around the chaos and touched the door, practically caressing it. Nothing around me mattered although deep down, I knew the sensation I was experiencing was, under the circumstances, wrong… almost sensual. I studied every nook and cranny of the door's design. Somehow, I identified a problem with the overall fit. I continued to study it in the hopes I would identify what my gut feeling was telling me, but I couldn't quite pinpoint it. The wrought iron circular handle and escutcheon fitted by Noah were perfectly suited but there was something amiss. I pulled the key from the lock and stroked it before concentrating on the attached silver chain. The chain was of a length that could, if required, be attached to an apron string or even worn around the wrist. I detached the chain from the key and linked the two ends together before trying it on. With it in place, I lifted my arm to admire what now looked like a purpose made bracelet. It was only as I stood back and unceremoniously trod on poor Noah's arm that I knew exactly what it was that was bothering me.

Before I could utter a word, I was abruptly dragged away and into the lounge by Joel, "Hey. What in hell were you thinking in there? The poor guy has enough to cope with, without you adding insult to injury."

He was right of course, although it still did not alter the passage of my thoughts as I said something strange, "It's the hinges, they're all wrong. They look wrong don't they? They should be heavy-duty decorative 'T' hinges. We'll have to get some. Yes. We'll need three."

Joel guided me to the sofa, "I think you had better get some medical help. No, better still, I'll call for a psychiatrist."

I suddenly snapped out of my trance-like state. On realisation I apologised for my lack of care, "I'm sorry Joel. I seem to have been babbling like an idiot. Perhaps it's the shock of seeing what's going on. I don't understand what happened in there with Noah and Rodney. Oh, I don't know. Perhaps…" I left it there as the doctor poked his head around the corner, "We're taking these two to the hospital. Sorry about the mess but we don't have time to clear up. Can't really make out who to contact since the lad isn't making much sense. We need…" He paused slightly, "…a next of kin and all that. Could you do the honours?"

Joel and I spoke in unison, "Next of kin?!"

The doctor quickly clarified his comments, "Oh, nothing to worry about. They are both stable. We just need to let their nearest and dearest know where they are, that's all. Bye." With that, he was gone, leaving us with nothing more than the sounds of the metallic clattering of equipment and confusion.

Not knowing what to do, Joel took command, "Right, you ring Bill's wife… Ida, isn't it? Yes, I think that's what it was; Ida. I'll sort out the kitchen guy." Commandingly, he thrust my phone into my hands. Immediately, I started to dial the number as if on autopilot.

"Oh! Hello Bill. Sorry, I expected Ida to answer. I hope you are well… anyway, it's Claire here. Just to let you know that Rodney has been taken to hospital." Bill started to panic on the other end of the 'phone, "Oh, no, no, no, I don't think it's that bad. But, he will probably need stitches."

"What hospital?" Bill asked.

"Oh, the doctor didn't say. I guess they'll be going to the one nearest because of the heart attack."

"Heart attack?!" Bill exclaimed.

"Oh! No, it wasn't Rodney who had the heart attack. Oh dear, I'm sorry."

I ended the call without adding anything more since I sounded like I was making matters worse. Joel, on the other hand, had done better since he had prepared himself.

When he had finished, I asked him how he knew who to contact, "Simple…, the firm's details are on the plans in the kitchen. So, all I had to do was phone the office. I spoke to a nice sounding guy who said I was lucky since he had just happened to call in for some tools. He said the guy who had the heart attack must be Noah and he would call his wife to let her know." Joel unexpectedly leaned forward and caressed the chain wrapped around my wrist. Before adding, "Strange, isn't it? The dream I mean."

I merely nodded and cuddled into him for comfort.

It took time for me to recover before I could go into the kitchen. Joel had done a remarkable job of clearing up and interestingly, I surveyed my new kitchen for the first time. My eyes were drawn to the washing machine and I rushed over to retrieve my jeans. I found them and carefully untangled them from a mix of other items before searching the pockets. Thankfully, the necklace was still there and none worse for wear. In fact, if anything, the necklace appeared to glisten, just as the bracelet appeared to glow too. Unceremoniously, I dropped the jeans onto the floor and put the necklace around my neck where it hung low and between my cleavage. For some reason, the feeling I was now experiencing was little short of euphoria. For once, I didn't centre my attention on the back door as I playfully opened and closed all of the 'soft close' drawers and cupboards, whilst admiring the rest of the gleaming fixtures and fittings.

The revamped Aga looked magnificent and blended in well with the newness of the other features. It wasn't long though, that I concentrated my gaze on the back door and studied its design as if it was the first time I had ever seen it. It now reminded me of a Spanish medieval gate I had once seen, but on a far smaller scale. On closer inspection, I discovered there were, indeed, small indentations down one side of the door. These indicated where three hinges were previously fitted. Furthermore, when I stood back, I could see the faintest of outlines depicting where the hinges were once attached. By visually tracing the full length and thickness of its design, I was able to get a better impression of their size and shape. I approached the door once more and gently ran my index finger over the small indentations. Now, more than ever, I was determined to find the right style hinges and have them fitted. I stood back again and could clearly imagine what it would have looked like when it was originally fitted. It was only now, though, that I wondered why it had been boarded up in the first place.

Why would somebody choose to close off such a practical entrance to the beautiful garden?

For now, I was just pleased to see it there… proud and functional.

Chapter 15

Relapse

After Joel had gone to bed, I spent hours pondering the last few days. Here, on the sofa, I felt good as the cottage now felt complete. Occasionally, I would unconsciously bring the angel pendant up to my mouth where I would sensuously rub it across my lips. The more I did this, the better it felt and the warmer the bracelet got too.

My mind drifted…

With the morning light came a shrill and insistent ringing. This persistent sound started as a dream and eventually became a reality. I picked up my mobile and, at first, tried to focus on the number before answering. Dazed, I said, "Hel...?" It was Bill's wife, Ida. Without waiting for me to finish speaking she told me that Noah had survived his ordeal, although it was 'touch and go' for a while. Also, and apparently, Rodney was a frequent visitor to the hospital. According to Ida, all was now okay. She reassured me Rodney was no worse for wear and was proud to be sporting yet another scar. I asked her if she could throw any light on what had happened, but she said she was unable to help. I thanked her for the call and hung up before looking at the glowing display on the phones small screen - the time was 11:30.

Still dressed from the day before, I got up and went into the kitchen where I found the backdoor wide open. Something felt wet beneath my feet and looked down to see a trail of muddy footprints. These led into the lounge and up the stairs. The trail finished at the foot of Joel's bed where I found him lying face down, naked. His feet were covered in mud, right up to the ankles where scratches were clearly visible on his lower legs. Carefully, I covered him up as he muttered and fidgeted in his slumber. As I did so, he turned to me and with just the whites of his eyes showing he said, *"You mustn't invite her in!"* With that, his body relaxed as he seemingly drifted off peacefully while I withdrew.

The hairs on the back of my neck stood up and an icy chill in the room made its way up from my toes to my crown of my head. I tried to back away from him and gasped as cold air now reached my lungs. My breath could be seen hanging in the air as if I were outside on a frosty morning. Once again, I tried to move my legs but they felt like lead, just as the light around me started to drain away. With all my strength and concentration working together, I managed to move backwards but everything remained sluggish. Even if I'd wanted to run, I couldn't. It took every ounce of my being to reach the door, and only then did some warmth and my feelings return. I eventually managed to move to the sanctuary of the lower ground and away from the cause of this phenomenon… namely Joel.

Drained of all energy, I sat on the bottom step of the stairs and occasionally looked over my shoulder as I felt the presence move closer. I looked up and could see nothing but darkness, as it started to creep down the stairs. With my remaining strength, I moved to the sofa where I collapsed in exhaustion. With what little strength I had left, I turned to face the stairs. From here, I could keep a close eye on the darkness as it crept down… nearer and nearer. With a need for comfort, I brought my legs up to my chest and rested my chin on my knees. My natural instinct was fear, but I tried to be analytical, tried to evaluate what was happening. Impulsively, I reached for the necklace and as I felt its presence, the darkness began to withdraw. With the heat coming from both the necklace and the bracelet, the apparition began to fade… first to grey, then to nothingness.

Still holding the pendant, I rose and slowly ventured up the stairs but feared every step, wondering what I might find up there. There to greet me, was nothing but light and warmth. I edged into Joel's room... here he was, by now, at rest and was actually snoring. I left him in peace, still convinced he was responsible for the unexplained event, although I did start to question my own sanity. I also questioned if his recent illness had triggered some form of phenomenal event. Although, in truth, I couldn't find an earthly reason how this could come about. There were also the stark warnings I was getting. Three times prior to today, I had heard the same warning, which made me think that the other times, although still slightly questionable, were real.

I made sure Joel was comfortable and looked around to see if anything was out of place. Nothing stood out.

Eventually, I returned to the kitchen and fully regained my composure. Here I reached to close the door. Something caught my eye and I stopped short. From where I stood, I could clearly see Joel's footprints leading inwardly from outside. Curiosity caused me to follow them as far as the stream. From where I stood, I could clearly see the path he took. It showed he had crossed the stream at the point where the bridge once stood. The other side was almost as obvious since the meadow plants were completely flattened in places. I took a running jump and just made it across the stream and into the meadow. The trail thinned out by the bench where I sat feeling the cool breeze on my body. From where I sat, I looked up at the bedroom window and from within, I swore I saw something move. I shuffled in my seat and purposefully looked to the ground.

I hadn't noticed Joel's hands since they were underneath his body when I found him, but the ground around me showed very distinct signs of digging and scraping with fingers. Nothing here made sense either, so I got up and made my way back into the house. I boiled the kettle with the intention of making coffee, knowing I would have to wake Joel and tackle him about his behaviour. By observing his responses, I might be able to come to some sort of conclusion, but I wasn't holding out much hope. There was a part of me, which wanted me to believe that what had happened had nothing to do with him. Somehow though, I wanted to place the blame squarely on his shoulders. This thought made everything more believable and, to a degree, better for me to cope with. But why did I want to feel this way? Why did I want to blame Joel? Only time would tell.

With trepidation and two cups of coffee in my hand, I headed back to Joel's room to confront him about the matter. As I entered his room I found Joel standing before me, head down but still naked with his hands by his side. He suddenly clamped his dirt-encrusted hands over his face. He sounded frightened as he said, "Cookie? I know you are there. I can't see anything. I'm blind. For fuck's sake... I'm blind! I'm blind and my head... I have a splitting headache!"

He then screamed.

Terrified, I dropped the cups and without hesitation, ran downstairs to call the only person I could think of, "Hello Suzy, it's me Claire..., yes..., well no, it's Joel, he said he has gone blind and has a headache. What should I do?"

Suzy reassured me that all would be well and said she would call for an ambulance as it sounded like he needed immediate medical care. I was about to give her the address when I realised she probably already had it, but prompted her just the same.

In reality, I had waited less than 15 minutes for the ambulance to arrive but in my mind, it seemed like an eternity. I was shaking as I tried to comfort Joel. Still in the clothes I had slept in, I met the ambulance and spoke to the driver while the paramedics saw to Joel. Joel, now wrapped in a blanket, was led to the vehicle as I got into the Golf. The ambulance stopped briefly in a layby about a mile up the road, before putting on the blue lights and roaring off. Initially, the speed of this event left me behind and I wasn't sure which hospital they were taking Joel to. There was no way I was going to keep up with the ambulance but for a while, I tried my best. I eventually lost sight of it as it exited a roundabout but by now, I had picked up the signs for the local hospital and parked in the visitor's car park.

I rushed into the A & E department, and unfamiliar with the surroundings, instantly felt lost. Although the ambulance was still outside with the back doors fully open, there was no sign of Joel or the crew. Once again, I found myself in a strange location with no idea what to do. I made enquiries but was told rather firmly to sit and wait.

Within an hour, I felt utter relief as I looked up and saw Suzy walking through the main entrance, carrying a thick folder clearly marked Joel D'Arcy, "Hello Claire, I was worried this might happen again." Suzy gently guided me to a quiet corner and away from the main entrance, "My bosses at Poole Hospital have allowed me to travel up to speak with the consultant here since I know Joel and understand his case notes. Look..., to be honest, I chose to come here since I have taken a personal interest in Joel's case. I shall do all I can to..."

With her kind words and my recent turmoil back at the cottage, I felt close to tears. Suzy guided me to a nearby seat and listened as I explained, "He said he was blind. Where have they taken him?"

With that, Suzy got up to see if she could find out what was going on. It wasn't long before she came back with a caring smile on her face, "He's in good hands, but I'm afraid he will have to stay here for a while. Look, I know it is going to be difficult but try not to worry too much. There is nothing we can do at this stage but I understand the signs are positive, although you must realise that it is still early days."

There was no choice but for me to go back home.

Chapter 16

A Visitor

With sheer willpower and dogged determination, I managed to bring the doll's house down from the loft and struggled with it into the kitchen. It was extraordinarily heavy, almost as if it had something hidden within. I eventually placed it on top of the small square kitchen table, which was what I'd had to settle for as a compromise for the door being hung. Although the table was substantial in structure, it creaked under the weight and just managed to support the doll's house. It was only now that I pondered how I had actually managed to get it to where it now stood. Quickly putting that to one side, I eagerly looked it over and marvelled at the sheer intricacy of its design.

What happened next came as rather a shock to me as I opened the frontage for the first time. All the features I currently had in the house were replicated, right down to the last detail. I put my hand to my mouth and stepped back as I looked at the style, colour and position of the furniture within. It wasn't just similar... *It was exact*! Even the walls had been painted in the same colours, right down to the unusual shade of blue I had chosen for the front room. My mind wandered as I tried to reason with the reality of it all before coming to the only conclusion I could. I determined, and much to my relief, that Joel had planned this as a surprise for me. Yes, that was it! Joel had craftily replaced the original furniture with what I now saw. Yes, I thought, it was his style to do something like this. Of course, he managed to save the last drops from the recently discarded paint pots to use on the tiny walls. With this conclusion drawn, I felt comfortable and even pleased by his efforts. His attention to detail was extraordinary... right down to the vase of flowers.

In truth, my assumption that Joel had any part to play in its creation was wrong. This could not have been the case since with hindsight, I now realise that the used paint tins were recently taken away with the general rubbish collection, and well before Joel had even returned from hospital. More importantly, and apart from that, I can't see how he had the time or effort to get into the loft without me knowing. Even the flowers I had been given had died extremely quickly through lack of water, and were removed before Joel could have seen them. In addition, there was the time factor to take into account. These points, although not subtle, had all but escaped me... perhaps my mind set preferred it that way.

I ventured closer and managed to look straight through the house just as the sun streamed through the back window. For a fleeting second I swear I saw, through the coinciding window, the back garden where I could see a young girl standing in the meadow looking straight at me. Once again, I backed up before quickly returning to have another look. There was nothing to be seen, certainly, nothing to suggest what I saw was real. My imagination was now running wild and guessed this had something to do with the trauma I had recently gone through with Rodney and Noah, and now Joel again. Perhaps, thinking on, my mind was tricked by the suddenness of the light that had flooded through the window and into the kitchen.

On closer inspection, I looked at the miniature studded backdoor, which clearly revealed three decorative T hinges. With a certain amount of guile and patience, I copied the design onto a piece of paper before measuring the details I had found on the door itself. Pleased with my endeavours, I placed the piece of paper into my bag and headed for the door. Without thought, I got into the car and headed for Salisbury town centre.

It wasn't until I parked in Endless Street that I realised I hadn't a clue where I was going or exactly what I was looking for. I had already made numerous enquiries before I came across an old man sitting with his dog. His kindly face did not mirror the aggression of his elderly dog who seemed content on snapping at my ankles, "Maggs leave the poor girl alone. Sorry..." He said as he added, "I don't know what's got into her. Get down Maggs." With that, he shortened her lead, which would have allowed me past the narrow pathway without stepping into the road.

I stopped short and asked the pertinent question, "I'm sorry, but can you help me? I am trying to locate a place that would be able to make me a couple of wrought iron hinges. Yes, I guess they would be made of that."

The old man pulled Maggs even closer and asked me to sit next to him, which I politely refused, "Oh!" He said, disappointed, "Well, you'll be wanting Martyn then. 'Jack's Bush Forge', but you'll have to travel a bit coz his place is a ways from here you know. Known him since he were a lad I have." I felt unsure about the way Maggs was looking at me, which made me feel very nervous as I tried to encourage the man to give me the vital information I needed. Unfortunately, he seemed to relish my company, and I also got the impression he wanted somebody to talk to, "Arnold, that's my name…, and yours?" He asked politely.

"Oh, Claire… How do you do Arnold?"

He offered his hand but Maggs seemed to warn me off with a short, sharp bark. Arnold's smile revealed several missing teeth, "Sorry about that, I don't know what's come over her." He quickly changed the subject, "I've lived here 84 years man and boy, and never met a Claire before." He chuckled, "Anyhow, from here…" He stood, turned and pointed, "…you want to make your way up to the A30 and then take the A343. Now this is the difficult bit, if you reach Hollom Down Road, which will be on your right, then you have gone too far coz that'll take you back to the A30. Now if you see Big Ben then you've definitely gone too far." He chuckled heartily.

His laughter was infectious as I too found myself giggling at his little joke. Even Maggs seemed to relax as her grey muzzle stopped twitching and no longer seemed to express the need to take a bite out of me.

I eventually bid Arnold farewell and proceeded to seek out 'Jack's Bush Forge' and Martyn. It didn't take long for me to find Martyn's forge, although finding it was made slightly more difficult due, partly, to the thick undergrowth surrounding the building. Oddly, I felt a twinge of anguish as I passed the road that would have led back to my home. If only I had known! All I had to do was to turn right at the end of the main road leading from my house and take a left. This route would have taken me straight to Martyn's property.

The thought of the distance I had just travelled relative to Rose Cottage made me consider my latest course of action. Seemingly, I had once again put to the back of my mind Joel's condition and placed a stronger emphasis on such trivial features as hinges. Somehow though, my mind shifted from one extreme to another and without thought of the consequences.

The forge was not what I had expected, since my only other experience dealing with a blacksmith was when I was much, much younger and had a pony. During this short-lived phase, I visited a 'Smithy' who worked out of a ramshackle, almost derelict shed to have the pony shod. The purpose built building I was now standing in was immaculate, and dare I say, well designed by comparison.

The man standing next to the forge was deep in reflexion when I arrived, and was measuring a length of metal rod. I stepped forward and pronounced myself loudly by issuing a loud cough.

He jumped as he became aware of my presence, "Good grief, sorry! I'm sorry. You rather caught me off guard. How can I help you?"

His politeness made my task somewhat easier, "No, no, I should be the one to apologise. Are you Martyn?"

He nodded before putting out his hand then immediately withdrawing it without contact after noticing how dirty it was. He quickly picked up a cloth and began to wipe his hands, "Yes, Martyn at your service. How can I help you?" He repeated.

I scrabbled around in my bag trying to find the small piece of paper and ended up almost tipping everything out. Finally, I found the paper and handed it to him.

Martyn studied the freehand drawing and the dimensions, "How many?" He asked politely.

"Three to the exact design, please." I answered confidently.

He took a step or two backwards to be nearer the light from behind him, "Three, eh! Well I have a big job on at the moment, although I've almost finished. Well, let me see. How about next Thursday? I can have them ready for you to pick up by mid-afternoon, if that is okay with you?"

This was sooner than I had expected and readily agreed without even asking for a price. Martyn looked at me as I was about to leave before asking, "I'll need your details. Oh, and do you wanted them painted? And don't you want you want to know how much?"

Given the option, I somehow had the feeling that the hinges should remain unpainted and declined on that basis. At his behest, I agreed on a coat of flat black undercoat. Finally, we negotiated a price and after giving him my details, I left feeling more than happy with the arrangements.

The trip home was made much easier since I now knew exactly where I was.

As I entered the house, I could smell something very disturbing, before being confronted by a large swarm of black flies. A quick search was made easier by following the trail of the offending smell, which revealed a disgusting find. In the centre of the kitchen was a dead black cat with some of its entrails spread away from the animal and towards the backdoor. But there was something else, and my head started to spin when I bent down to have a closer look. There was a name scrawled on the floor in, I assume, the cat's blood… MARCIE! I heaved, jumped up and made a dash for the kitchen sink. After a moment or two, shaking, I tied a tea towel around my nose and the lower part of my face before finding a plastic bin liner. I didn't know what to think, I just needed to get this mess out of my kitchen immediately. Carefully, I placed the bag over rotting remains and scooped them into the bag. I took it outside at arm's length. Not sure what to do with it, I decided to bury it as far away from the house as I could. I couldn't deal with the implications of finding a name written in blood on the floor just at that moment. I just knew I had to get that dead animal away from the house.

After locating a spade in the ramshackle shed, I decided on a spot on the other side of the stream. I threw the spade across the stream and jumped the span with the bin liner swinging freely. As I landed, the bag slapped against my leg and split open, which was to give me a greater shock than anything I could have anticipated. The cat's remains fell out and hit the ground. Suddenly, it started to move in a trembling, vibrating sort of way before it yowled in a terrible, ear piercing pitch. Its quivering body stretched as its tail thrashed from side to side, before getting to its feet. Within moments, it ran towards the copse with its innards still trailing. Horrified, I slipped backwards and fell into the stream. For the first time, I became aware of the true depth of the water and swore as I climbed out. To make matters worse, I found myself still on the 'wrong' side of the stream but now with sodden clothes. Straightaway I made an exerted effort to get to the right side.

Greatly shaken by what had just taken place I felt, once more, physically sick. Dishevelled, I started to run back to the house. I entered the kitchen, now at my wits ends at the thought of having to clean up the floor and that…name. Gingerly I stepped through the door and gasped since there were no flies, no blood, and not a single sign of any of the horror I had just seen. The only thing I could see that was out of place was the backdoor on the doll's house… it was wide open.

Still traumatised by what had happened, I stripped off and removed the sagging tea towel from around my neck, before unceremoniously throwing the lot into the sink where it could stay for the foreseeable future. I made my way upstairs and got into the shower where I leaned against the tiles and tried to make sense of it all. I had to admit that there was no apparent reason for what had happened. As hard as I tried to find an explanation, I couldn't come to any conclusion. This time I couldn't blame poor Joel and even felt remorse for placing any blame on him in the first place. There was now more guilt on my part.

There was no saying how long I had been in the shower but it was obviously a long time as the bathroom had completely steamed up. Cautiously, I felt for the towels and briefly touched something solid I couldn't identify. I felt again and once I had the towel in my hand, I quickly wrapped myself up and shivered, out of both cold and dread. As the steam evaporated, I searched for anything out of the ordinary, but couldn't find a thing. I felt exhausted and ran into my bedroom where I felt safe. I took my time drying, before dusting myself down with talcum powder. As soon as I got dressed I felt more in control of the situation. I re-entered the bathroom and had another good look around. I needed to see if I could find evidence of what I had touched when I reached for the towel. There was nothing... in fact; there was nothing at all that obstructed the space between the shower and the towel rail.

Warily, I cleared up the bathroom. Afterwards, I went back into the bedroom only to find yet another mystery. There were footprints in the talcum powder residue left on the floor. They were clearly not mine, since they were much smaller. The small steps led toward the window and that is where they stopped. Slowly, I followed them. The garden looked peaceful, as a light wind made the tall flowers and grasses sway almost mystically. My eye ventured further into the distance and I spotted what I thought could be an answer to my recent problems.

It took me several minutes, but I managed to catch up with the sheep farmer I had fleetingly seen from time to time. I was confident I had found the perpetrator of all my recent grief. It never came into my mind how he was creating such illusions or how he could create such perfect footprints in a size obviously not his own. I shouted at him, "Oi! I want a word with you." My adrenalin was running high, although my facts were rather minimal. For some reason the man refused to stop. In fact he sped up, which caused me to run after him. Determined, I felt angry at his evasion and wanted to confront him. Before I could get too close though, I found myself flanked by two dogs who appeared agitated by my presence. I felt threatened and stopped immediately with the feeling of impending harm. I searched for the farmer, and then I saw him with his head tilted down. He stopped in his tracks and turned my way, although I was unable to see his face immediately. There was a sharp whistle and the dogs turned and ran. Shaken, I pressed on and ranted for a while as he slowly lifted his head. I was horrified by what I saw and stopped talking as a result. Deeply embedded scarring had horrifically turned half of his face into an appalling mess of dark red skin. I recognised the scars as those caused by fire.

A few distorted words formed in my head, only to be stifled in my throat. The man was now looking at me fully, although I was unsure if he was blind in his damaged right eye. As if I had not had enough shocks today, this just about finished me off, and I fainted.

I came to in a barn and felt very vulnerable as I looked around to see the man sitting just a few metres away. He did not seem threatening, but I knew it would be prudent to be cautious. I stood and gave the impression that I was dusting myself down but was, in reality, feeling for any sort of impropriety. Certain nothing had happened, and I started to slowly head for the door whilst apologising. The man spoke with a rich and velvety voice, "No, don't be sorry, it is not your fault. There are not that many people who can look at me and not be disgusted by what they see. Even into my good eye..." He laughed without conviction, "Well, I know how hideous I look." There was no way I could deny his words, but almost said the false and empty words that some use when they see awful scaring like this... that he wasn't hideous but the truth is he was. Although there was his velvet sounding voice, which was almost mesmerising.

Perhaps it was the appeal of his voice that gave me the confidence to speak out so bluntly, I whispered, "What happened to you? I mean..."

I didn't need to finish the sentence and the man wasn't going to let me, "Fire. Come here and sit down."

My response was somewhat insensitive, "I gathered that... what I meant was..."

His response was sharp, and rightly, so, "I know what you meant!"

We both apologised at the same time. The apologies seemed to put us both in a better frame of mind. With that, he pointed to an upturned tea chest where I sat feeling more relaxed the more he spoke, "Seeing that there is a connection between the two of us, I feel comfortable enough to mention a few things." His sentence confused me, as I could see no connection to him other than the few brief, if not, isolated meetings since I discovered Rose Cottage. He continued, "I don't talk to many people these days. In fact it is a wonder I still live around here since my…" He faltered for a while and unconsciously touched his face, "…since my 'accident' many years ago. You see, a local girl went missing and, I suppose, since I lived alone, people started to form various conclusions. The connection I had mentioned earlier was because of this and where you now live. One night I was in bed when I heard a noise downstairs and since my dogs did not bark I thought I should investigate. The intruders had killed my dogs. They killed them, but more than that, I quickly realised they had set fire to my place. They had somehow thought I had something to do with the girl's disappearance." He appeared to weep, although I saw no tears, "I was on the stairs seconds before they collapsed. The resulting fall did two things. Firstly, it took me, for a brief second, much closer to the fire hence…" Silently, he ran his hand over his face before continuing, "…and secondly, perhaps more fortunately, the heat of the fire had blown out the windows and I managed to escape quickly from the house. For my sins, and because of that, I am still here today. Nobody called for the fire brigade or an ambulance until the house was completely destroyed. Eventually, I was taken to Odstock Hospital and spent months there."

The phrase 'for my sins' appeared to indicate guilt. Was he confessing a sin? Although I really felt for him I sensed the need to know more about the little girl and was about to ask when I was interrupted, "I know what you are going to ask. Was it me? Did I have anything to do with her disappearance? That's what you were going to say wasn't it?" I merely nodded, "If it had been me, then this would have been well justified. As it happens, I was away when she vanished and it was soon proven that I had nothing to do with her disappearance. She was last seen leaving your house… Well, it's your house now. By the way, nobody was charged with what happened to me. There wasn't even a proper investigation into what happened at my place that night. No…" He paused briefly, "…by the time they confirmed my innocence," He laughed, "The trail, if you excuse the pun, had gone cold."

I no longer looked at him with revulsion, and felt that somehow sympathy would have been worse. For some reason I just listened to him and absorbed what he was telling me. I then took the rash and unusual decision to invite him back to the cottage for tea, which surprisingly he accepted, "I was going to escort you back anyways. He turned towards the door, "Can't trust everybody you meet." He chuckled.

When we left the barn, I found myself in a part of the copse I did not recognise, although to be fair I had not ventured too far into the woods… ever. To our right we passed the remains of a chimneystack covered in moss. This sight spoke volumes. He turned around and looked back at the barn, "That is where I live now. It's not much, but it is home and these days I don't get bothered."

He casually glanced at the ruins of his house as he led me back home, but remained silent as we walked on.

Chapter 17

Seeking Forgiveness

As we approached the cottage, my guest held back a little as he surveyed the scene, "Although I helped the guys get here when you moved in, I steered clear of the house because I am fearful of it." This begged me to ask why he had accepted my offer, "I don't really know. Perhaps it is because I trust you and know you had nothing to do with what happened to me, unlike that lot." His eye veered to the right as he made a gesture with his head indicating towards the village.

We took a few more steps forward when he stopped again and stared at the backdoor. He said nothing but there was a sign of recognition as something registered in his mind. Just before we reached the stream, I picked up the spade I had left there earlier. Carefully, I jumped the streams span, "I must get something done about that." I said nonchalantly.

As we entered the cottage, I felt embarrassed by the pile of clothes in the sink and tried to explain, "Oh, I'm sorry but there was this…" I then looked and saw my bra dangling over the side. By trying to retrieve it stealthily, I instead brought it to my guest's attention, "As I said, I'm sorry for the state of the place."

My guest chipped in, "Look, I'm sorry. This looks like a bad time for you, perhaps I should go."

I was adamant he should stay and insisted he should whilst deftly flicking my exposed bra into the sink and out of sight.

I looked at the floor to confirm if what I had seen earlier was real or not. Apart from the mess I had created throwing my clothes off, there was nothing out of the ordinary to see. Whilst I was clearing up and making tea, my guest looked at the newly fitted door with extreme interest and mumbled something. "Sorry?" I replied, "I didn't quite catch what you said."

He took his time answering, "Oh, nothing really. Although I do remember this door before it was oddly taken down. Miss Adams lived here then, and come to think about it… Yes, from memory, it was taken down soon after Julianne had disappeared."

He repeated her name and held it there for a moment or two before speaking again, "Julianne… That was the name of the girl who went missing." I admitted I knew of the girl since I had recently met with her Father. This brought a response I did not expect, "I feel for them. They did not deserve to lose her like that. We have all suffered terribly in our own ways after her disappearance and we all had a terrible grief to bear"

I looked up at him and no longer saw the dreadful scarring, but a man in turmoil. There was more to this story than I had initially believed and wanted to know more. "Tell me what you mean by that last statement."

There was another brief pause before he spoke again, "I suppose, when I killed my wife and daughter in a car crash, the people around here blamed me. She was a local girl and was loved by all, but none more so than by me. Just because I'd lost my own daughter…why would they assume I'd hurt someone else's? They seem to forget that…" It was obvious he was reliving a very painful time in his life. "I adored them both and when they died, I lost everything. My wife and daughter meant everything to me and now they are gone." He finished his sentence through gritted teeth, "And all because I lost concentration for a split second." He then bowed his head.

This explanation may well account for the earlier remark that had had me baffled. The phrase, 'for my sins' now began to make complete sense. I no longer pressed for answers, since there was nothing either of us could add. Delicately, I excused myself, leaving him standing in the kitchen still staring at the door. I left the room because I did not want him to see my tears. My actions were selfish and although I wanted to comfort him with kind words, I couldn't. I just couldn't find the right words to say… especially to a man who had gone through so much.

Eventually I returned and showed my guest into the lounge before I returned to the kitchen. Slightly flustered, I quickly busied myself by preparing a light snack to go with the tea I was brewing.

With the food and drink served, there was a period of silence. My guest suddenly got up and approached me, "Edward Crinchley!" He said and extended his left hand, which I readily accepted. I soon realised his right hand had also been badly disfigured by the fire thus explaining the left handed shake. He saw my gaze and looked down at it, "I've learned how to use it again, but I feel it offends some so I don't offer it. I mostly wear gloves but today…" He fell silent then pulled his hand out of sight as I said, "Claire…, Claire Chambers. I am pleased to meet you Mr Edward Crinchley."

For the first time I saw what I assumed was a smile, "How do Claire Chambers…, please call me Crinchley." He continued smiling as he sat, which made me feel slightly nervous, but conversely quite safe. It was extremely difficult to imagine what he had looked like before the fire but I could imagine he had been a handsome man.

I felt goose bumps creep up my spine as he caught me looking at him. It was as if he could read my mind, "All the photos showing how I once looked were destroyed in the fire." He looked pensive before adding, "What is sadder is that I no longer have the precious few photographs of…" He placed his left hand over his eyes and stopped talking.

I didn't know what to do. I was about to get up and comfort him but somehow felt that he would reject any physical response. In truth, I could not offer any form of consolation since I felt so odd about the situation. It wasn't long before he raised his head and apologised, to which I smiled telling him not to worry, since I knew how emotional these things could get. I stopped short of telling him what I had endured since because by doing so, I felt I would only be entering a 'who has suffered the most' competition. This was one such competition I could not win. Losing a Mother, Father, Nan or even a wife was terrible, but losing a child, in my mind, could not be compared.

There was another awkward silence for a while as I watched my guest slowly look around the room. He appeared to be taking in as many of the features as he could. His gaze was so intense that I'm sure if there were a cobweb in the room, then he had noted it.

It was a while before either of us spoke again, "Always wondered what it would be like. I mean, it's not what I imagined. I always thought there would be darkness in the heart of this old house." He looked up apologetically, "I'm sorry! I shouldn't express an opinion like that so openly. I of all, people know that rumours often have consequences."

I looked at him closely wanting to know what he meant by that, so I asked, "Is there a reason for this so-called darkness? Ever since I first came to this part of the country, I got the impression that there was something 'not quite right' about it. What rumours?"

Crinchley leaned back in his chair whilst doing his best to cradle the cup of tea, "Look, I'm sorry…, perhaps I should go."

I was not going to let him leave until he explained himself, "No!" I insisted, "I want to know the truth about this place - and it might help you if I first explained how I came to live here."

I explained everything, including a few of the weirder events I had encountered since I had moved in, but strangely not the most recent, which had caused me to confront him. This is also when I mentioned the day I viewed the cottage for the first time, "The sheep..." I said, "...You know, before I actually bought the cottage and I was here to view it. The way the sheep behaved. Do you remember?"

He nodded, "Yes! About that day, I don't know what happened and as I didn't want to get into any discussions with you all, I kept back. Strange that. Never seen anything like it before or since, and I have farmed sheep forever! Fairly spooked me if I'm honest. But once they were past the obstacle they returned to normal."

Being referred to as an 'obstacle' was one thing, but his admission that things weren't normal that day was curious. I agreed I didn't think their behaviour was usual and quickly dropped the subject. I was now convinced that Crinchley could have done nothing to prevent events on that day. This was an interesting point really, since although I had only just met him, I felt his integrity was no longer an issue. I suppose, similarly, neither was the integrity of Robin Alsford, whose daughter had disappeared all those years ago. Perhaps my mind had originally concluded that everybody who had an association with Rose Cottage had something to hide.

Yes… I think I now understood these two men.

During the ensuing discussions, I brought Joel into events. Strangely, it wasn't until then that I realised how I had again been reluctant to admit his existence. It was as if Rose Cottage was shielding me from his presence. My reasoning did not make sense, but I question what did make sense these days. As my guest was absorbing what I had told him, I got up and turned on two table lamps as the night had started to draw in. There was also a slight chill in the air and I excused myself once more so I could get something warm to put on. I found a sweater owned by Joel and as if by tribute to my lack of concern toward him, I put it on without hesitation. The large and baggy sweater felt good against my bare arms giving me the warmth and comfort I felt I needed.

When I returned to the room, I was astonished to see it empty. I looked around and reacted to a noise coming from the kitchen. I found Crinchley examining the back door, "It's not right you know. The hinges are all wrong. Look! See here. You can clearly see where the hinges were once fixed."

I explained the situation and showed him the doll's house whilst further explaining my clever little idea of recreating the original hinges. He seemed impressed.

I now urged him to explain his earlier comment about 'rumours'. "Have you something to tell me?" I asked, "I really need to know."

His response was as expected and somewhat slow in coming, "I suppose. You see, this house was built on the remains of another. One that was once thought to be involved in witchcraft." Despite the warmth of Joel's sweater, I felt the goose bumps appear on my arms and the hairs on the back of my neck bristled as if teased by electricity. I was determined to hear more, so I allowed him to continue without interruption, "The site was originally demolished in the early nineteenth century but not before the three so-called witches who lived there were put to death by scared locals." Crinchley then muttered something about knowing how they must have felt, which seemed quite valid under the circumstances. He continued, "They say that the mummified remains of a black cat were later found bricked up, BUT..." He dramatically emphasised the word 'BUT' by raising his good hand, "...once exposed to daylight, it is said that the cat returned to life and fled into the woods."

This part of the story bore too much resemblance to what had just happened to me. It was also a point I had not told Crinchley earlier because I thought he would not believe me. This was far too much for me to bear and my expression must have betrayed this as my guest suddenly said that he had to go. In some ways, I did not want him to go…, especially in light of this newfound information.

Although our meeting finished abruptly, Edward Crinchley promised to call back at some time in the near future. He knew I was about to press him for more information, but for now he had had enough…, and who could blame him?

As he left, he turned to me and in the half-light. From this angle, I could only see his 'good' side, which portrayed the man he once was. Yes, I concluded, he had once been extremely handsome.

I raised a hand in a small wave as he disappeared.

Chapter 18

Julianne

I tried to put the recent revelations to the back of my mind, but found it tough. It was also difficult for me to sleep that night and the morning couldn't have arrived quickly enough for my liking. But when I did sleep, my dreams that night reflected the stories I had heard. The faces of the people involved spun relentlessly around in my head. When I did fully wake, I found myself still wearing Joel's sweater, which was now drenched with perspiration, 'I suppose that's why they are called sweaters', I mumbled.

My feeble attempt at humour did nothing to stimulate the confidence I seemed to be lacking at that moment.

With great effort, I managed to get myself into a sitting position and onto the edge of the bed. It was only now that I remembered one of the most vivid of all of the dreams I had that night. With my hands pushing down on the mattress, arms straight and head leaning forward, I closed my eyes to recall one particular feature of the dream…, a face.

The girl's long blonde hair hung forward and partly covered her face. At first, I could not see her eyes but when I did, I was utterly stunned by their dullness. Being blue, they should have sparkled with life, but these eyes were dead, with no emotion or expression that would betray any inner feelings. It was then that she appeared to float back and away from me. Only then, did I see her in her entirety. Her feet pointed inwards and her shoes were clearly worn on one side, which suggested she had problems with her walking. I don't know why, but the clothes she wore were much more modern than I imagined they should be. Jeans, un-tucked red and white checked shirt covering what appeared to be a light blue t-shirt. Mostly, the clothes looked clean but there was something not quite right. At first, I could not quite grasp what that something was, and there seemed to be an awful smell that I couldn't place.

As she stared at me I tried to divert my eyes, but she seemed to have power over me. Her left hand reached for her neck and appeared to be toying with something invisible. As she did this, I found myself feeling for the angel necklace and realised what she was indicating. The dream then started to take on a much more macabre setting as I realised what exactly it was about her clothing that bothered me. Her clothes were moving in a strange way! Suddenly, from every pocket, opening and buttonhole appeared a series of insects - ranging from maggots, beetles and centipedes to earth worms. More alarmingly, as I watched in horror, more insects started to emerge… this time, from her bodily orifices. This happened just moments before her skin began to dissolve.

Desperately, I tried to look away but I couldn't… and then suddenly it was over.

Sure, I knew it was a dream that I was reliving, but everything seemed so real. The associated smell was rotting flesh… much like the cats! At first, it reached my nostrils as a sickly sweet aroma, before taking on a much more aggressive odour. I had only previously associated this odour with death. The smell did not immediately fade away and lingered in my nostrils for some time to come, long after the images had faded.

I put my hands to my face and looked at the grim reality of what was going on. I was still trying to convince myself that it was only a dream. Somehow though, I knew it was more than that.

There was a general feeling of uneasiness about me, so I got up and looked out of the window to seek calmness. My view of the surrounding area was limited though, as the cottage was shrouded in a ground mist. Even now, I began imagining things, as I became convinced I saw the mist move in an unusual way. It moved as if somebody invisible had walked through it and disturbed its stillness. A narrow path developed through the mist, and a swirling mass whipped itself up in a series of vortexes before quickly disappearing by the bench. This was doing nothing to calm my nerves but I stood motionless, just watching. I tried to convince myself that I saw nothing more than the result of a slight breeze…, albeit one isolated to the area directly surrounding the house.

Bizarrely, I then decided I would drive to the hospital to see Joel and, should he be awake, seek his total forgiveness. Surely, he must wonder about me sometimes. My apparent lack of concern could not have escaped his attention again, and I felt awful. As I left, I grabbed my phone and car keys but got no further than the front door. I heard a car approaching.

To my surprise, my visitor was none other than Suzy McMillan. My heart nearly stopped - it must be about Joel…

I approached the car, almost terrified, but was greeted by a welcoming smile, "Hi Claire, apologies for dropping by unannounced, but I have not been able to contact you by phone. Sorry, are you going somewhere?"

I took a quick look at my mobile to see if I had any missed calls. I had not and frowned when I noticed the lack of signal. I quickly explained that I was on my way to the hospital to see Joel. Suzy smiled and went on to tell me the latest news, "I'll try and make this simple and without sounding too dramatic. We are convinced Joel's condition was brought on by shock, so in that instance it is good news. His condition..."

This seemingly innocuous news somehow had an impact on my psyche, which manifested itself into a sudden bout of agitation. It didn't initially turn into a full panic attack, but her words caused me to gasp. Instinctively, I pressed my hand to my chest as if to check my breathing and heart rate. There was a moment when I could no longer control myself and began to quiver as the news struck home.

Perhaps I reacted the way I did due to my recent experiences, I don't know, but I was suddenly feeling very unwell.

The next thing I knew, I was being helped into the house by Suzy. Being the professional she was, she led me inside the house and to a seat, "I'll make some tea… Less caffeine than coffee. Where is the kitchen? Through here?" She pointed in the right direction and left the room. When she returned, she handed me a particularly weak and sugary mug of tea. It was of a consistency I would not normally drink but I hastily drank it.

My nerves were now truly shot to pieces. I then wondered if Joel's latest ailment had something to do with the condition he was in on the day I found him naked and caked in mud. I silently chastised myself, 'Stupid girl…, of course it did!'

Suzy elaborated on Joel's state of mind. Here, she assured me that he was doing well and should be released within a week. She added, "Mind you, that is if he continues to improve at the current rate." However, there was a surprise postscript added to this report, "I don't know how to tell you this…, but he has asked me to tell you something…" She hesitated, "He told me to tell you that he does not want to come back here. He asked…"

I then interrupted, "Whoa! Are you saying he doesn't want to see me? I know I have not been there for him like I should have done, but I didn't think he would not want to see me. I'm his best friend!" My tone was rather aggressive and, to a degree, overly defensive.

Suzy listened intently and let me rant on for a while before she coolly continued, "No, no… It's not you. In fact, he has asked if you would collect him next week and take him back to London. No, it's more to do with what he claims to have seen here." She paused again, this time observing her surroundings, "In truth, it is the real reason I came in the first place. You see, he claims to have seen a young girl rise out from the ground and ask him for help. Apparently, it was something he could not offer, although at the time he said he did try. I tried to explain to him that this manifestation could be a result of his recent condition, but he refused to believe it, saying that it felt too real to be a 'so-called' manifestation. Somehow, though, I believed him. He was very convincing and there was something in his voice. Yes. What he said and the way he put it was very believable."

This latest bit of news was more than I was prepared for, and with recent events still fresh in my mind, I confessed to Suzy just as I had with Crinchley about everything that had happened so far.

Suzy listened intently without showing any flicker of doubt before speaking, "Wow! With what you have told me, it does seem reasonable that Joel saw something. Although I must admit, your story is a bit scarier. Especially considering you have not had the same health problems that Joel has. What do you make of it?"

I got up, placed my empty mug on the small table next to a lamp, and asked Suzy to follow me. I gave her a tour of the house without answering her question. Why did I do this? Because I had no answer for her, and she didn't press for one. I showed her the room Joel was staying in, "This is where I found him on the day he told me he was blind." I then took her to my room and showed her the window, which looked down onto the garden. There was no sign of the mist I had seen earlier and the bench area was clear to see, "That is where I reckon he was digging with his bare hands." I pointed to emphasis the statement, although even from here it was plain to see the area Joel had been scraping with his hands. It then struck me how clear the site was from this raised position. I shrugged off my feeling of nervousness and took Suzy back downstairs.

Having Suzy here had already calmed my shot nerves so my next question seemed quite logical, "Suzy, do you have anywhere to stay tonight?" Her response was brief, "Well, I was on my way home." There was a pause as she understood what I was about to suggest, "Perhaps it is a good idea for me to stay here with you tonight, especially in light of what you have told me. I don't scare easy and might be able to help you make some sense of all of this…" She didn't seem to know how to finish her sentence and just smiled.

This would once again sound selfish, but Suzy's visit had unexpectedly solved two issues. I now knew how Joel was, and I also had the company I so craved after last night's events. Little did I know that tonight was going to be a trial all of its own.

The day quickly turned into evening and Suzy brought in what few belongings she had with her. We opened a bottle of wine to drink with our microwaved fish pie. Up until now, things had been calmer and the past events seemed… just that… past. Then Suzy said something that once again chilled me into becoming sober, "Did you know that Rose Cottage has its own place in hospital folk lore? Of course, I don't mean this Rose Cottage, I mean in general. You see, once upon a time, when there was a death on the ward, the Matron or Sister would call down to the porters and say 'One for Rose Cottage', which meant…" I got the meaning and Suzy must have seen something in my face that betrayed this, she stopped talking. But my tears came all the same.

After a while, I calmed down. I felt silly and apologised before suggesting that the wine had more to do with my tears than anything else.

My reluctance to go to bed was purely based on the recent dreams I had been having, but since I was so tired, both mentally and physically, I knew I must try. Suzy went up first while I pottered around clearing up. I looked at the kitchen clock and groaned as I noted the time… ten past one. With everything tidy, I turned around to head for the door, only to be confronted by the same sight that I couldn't shake from my mind earlier.

This time, I knew I wasn't dreaming.

The little girl, Julianne, was standing directly behind, and in-between the door and me. She was trying to say something whilst clutching at her blackened neckline where it was obvious her necklace had once proudly hung. Her body was in a further state of decomposition than when I last saw her… and I must admit I was frightened.

Frozen to the spot, I wanted to look away but couldn't, since my feet felt as if they were firmly glued to the floor. My tongue seemed to swell, and my skin became clammy and cold, and every hair on my body reacted to that strange sense of electricity drifting in the air. I cannot remember breathing, but I knew even this was becoming a problem too. Then, all of a sudden, there was a remarkable period of calm as my body started to relax, which unfortunately included my bladder. I felt the wetness flow down the inside of my right leg and onto my foot before seeping around the base of both feet. The subtle warmness was almost reassuring until I felt a slight breeze, which chilled my inner thigh, lower leg and feet. This almost degrading act didn't seem to bother me as much as it should have done, as I watched the girl intently. Her body had decayed badly but I was no longer afraid, mainly because of the look in her eyes. Her eyes and the surrounding area seemed to be oblivious to the putrefaction of the rest of her body. Her eyes told me not to be afraid. As I looked on, her partially exposed jawbone started to move up and down. Although there was no sound coming from her, I rather understood what she was trying to say. Slowly, I took off the necklace and held it towards her now outstretched hand. I held my breath as I stretched forward. My hand by now was shaking so much it caused the chain to swing mesmerizingly from side to side. As I held it the full distance away from my body, I started to sway, almost in tune with the motion of the necklace. She gently grasped the necklace but could not hold onto it as it passed between her decaying fingers. Remarkably, the angel pendant started to glow as it passed right through her hand. As it did so, it caused an amazing transformation to take place. Within moments, her body started to reanimate and became complete again. Likewise, her clothing became brighter and the frayed fabrics became new once more. She became more transparent but conversely, more defined in detail. Her smile was bewitching and most unlike the first time I had seen her. Now her eyes shone with… Well, they now shone with *life*.

I let the necklace go completely and it continued down to the solid floor. My gaze went with it. I followed it as it bounced backwards towards me and into the puddle of water surrounding my feet. By the time I looked up, Julianne was gone.

Eventually, I was able to move, but as I did, I slipped backwards on the wet floor and hit the ground with a jolt.

I felt embarrassed, uncomfortable and shaken as I sat in the sogginess, but not scared… not now. As I retrieved the necklace, I knew there was only one thing left to do, but first I needed to get cleaned up.

Chapter 19

Tears And Lies

No, I did not feel scared about any of the manifestations I had seen recently. There no longer seemed to be malevolence about the situation but calmness, and interestingly a purpose to which I was a key figure.

However, there was one more bizarre event that happened that night, and one, which I never even confessed to Suzy. At the top of the stairs, as I headed to the bathroom I was confronted by her. It was obviously from her stance that she was in some form of trance. Her face was pinched and brow furrowed with an intensity I had never seen before. Inexplicably, she spoke in a voice I recognised… A man's voice, *"You mustn't invite her in!"* I wanted to ask to whom she was referring. Just like the others who had given me the same warning, I knew I wouldn't get an answer. Strangely, it wasn't the warning that caused me the most anguish, but hearing my Dad's voice for the first time in ages, this was, by far, the most poignant of the situation. I stood once again, hardly able to breathe, let alone speak. Suzy turned and went back into the bedroom, and I went into mine. I climbed into bed too exhausted to cry or think. I must have fallen asleep immediately.

This latest event sparked a particular realisation in me. Over the last few months, in fact ever since I became involved with Rose Cottage, my outlook on life had changed. Even my temperament had changed and I had become much more emotional, which was way out of character for me. But I was convinced it was happening for a reason, and determined now to take control of the situation.

It was quite late in the day when Suzy finally rose from bed and came down to tea and toast. I asked her if she had slept well, to which she said something I found both amusing and unfortunate, "I slept like the dead!" To add to this she said something quite revealing, and almost confirmed what had happened during the night, "I know this sounds strange but do you have anything for a sore throat? For some reason my voice seems a little strained and my throat is pretty tender."

As she left, Suzy told me not to worry about a thing and departed not realising what I had been through and left, not knowing of the events I had recently endured. I didn't even tell her about the role she had played that night.

My aim now was to go to see Joel and build some bridges, knowing I could not tell him too much about what was going on at the cottage.

Before that though, I needed to do something for Julianne and headed straight for her parents' house.

Robin greeted me warmly, and took me into the kitchen of their cramped cottage to meet Liz. The warmth coming from the Aga was quite heady and the smell of freshly baked bread was divine. As I sat, I thought about my approach and for some reason decided, that today wasn't the day to tell them about my recent experience. I knew the bench and surrounding area in my garden had some connection to Julianne's disappearance, but didn't know how to approach the subject with my hosts. Perhaps I was deterred by the peace and tranquillity of their warm kitchen, I don't know.

Liz was slightly shorter than I was and her long, fair hair reminded me of Julianne's. In fact, meeting her was quite a shock. The more I studied her, the stronger the resemblance became. This similarity caused a shiver to shoot down my spine. Liz noticed me studying her and unconsciously touched her hair, which she then brought forward slightly. She smiled, "Sorry, I wasn't expecting visitors and haven't had time to put on my face." I, in turn, apologised and told her that I thought her hair was pretty, to which she merely smiled. Her smile hid something I could not have understood but was soon to find out, "My hair is all I have left to remind me of my daughter…"

I then said the most incredibly stupid thing I could, which brought silence to us all, "She also has your eyes."

Robin was the first to eventually speak, "How do you…, I don't understand."

Robin looked very bewildered as a tear streaked its way down his wife's left cheek, "Robin! What did she mean by that?" Robin looked at her sympathetically and walked toward her before clutching her arm. He then stooped and cradled her head into his shoulder before gently patting her back.

Her sobs were pitiful, and although my decision was not to say anything about recent events, I now felt I had to say something, "I'm sorry Mrs Alsford, Mr Alsford, but there is something I think you both should know."

She stopped crying and managed an apologetic smile whilst wiping her eyes. Alternatively, the look

I got from Robin reminded me of the glares I had been party to before we formally met. This wasn't what I had expected! It wasn't supposed to be like this. I was now quicker to explain, in part, the reasons for my statement, "I am so very, very sorry for upsetting you. That was the furthest thing from my mind. You see… Oh, dear I don't know where to start. You see, I dreamt about her and could clearly see what she looked like."

There was a certain amount of incredulity on the two faces before me, but their looks betrayed something I had not expected. Both appeared to relax a little and Liz asked me to tell her all about the dream and my interpretation of it.

We all sat down, and with a renewed confidence I finally did what I had originally intended to. Slowly, I pulled the necklace out of my pocket and handed it to Liz. At first, she could not accept the significance of what she had in her hand but when she did, she took in a deep breath. Her immediate reaction was to put the hand holding the necklace close to her chest and her other to her mouth. She gasped, "Where did you get this?"

At first, Robin didn't know where to look until finally, he fixed his gaze on me, "Did you find it at the house? You know this is… or was Julianne's, don't you?"

I nodded on both counts before adding, "She was wearing it in my dream." There was no reason for me to lie but I felt compelled to do so. It was almost as if I was trying to protect them from the truth and in this instance, I felt the truth about her state in the dream would have been too much.

There was a period of mixed emotions as all three of us digested what had just happened. For me it was cathartic, whilst for Liz and Robin it had opened a renewed bout of questions. Robin started, "Did you find it in the loft room?" I shook my head. Although it would have been simpler to tell them the truth, I initially remained mute on this particular subject. The rest of the questions were simpler to answer, although Robin's last statement had me baffled, "The last thing she told us on the day she disappeared was that she was going to help clear out their loft."

With his words ringing in my ears my brain snapped into gear, "*Their* loft? I thought a single lady lived there!?"

Robin stopped and thought for a while, "Did I say 'their'? Well I meant to say *the* loft..." He looked at his wife quizzically as he asked, "Did I really say *their* loft? Why would I say that?" He shrugged his shoulders before continuing, "Well... was it in there?"

I shook my head once more before lying again, "In the larder." For some reason this sounded right to me, and since I found the key to the back door there, the lie also seemed relevant.

There were no more questions after that. There were just tears and the occasional 'thank you' coming from my hosts. Liz brushed the hair away from her eyes and exhibited a look of youth as she placed the necklace around her own neck. This, in turn, brought a huge smile from Robin as he looked into his wife's eyes and gave her a kiss on her cheek. He then turned to me, "Thank you…, and I'm sorry about earlier. I don't mean earlier today, I mean when you first arrived in the village."

Robin's thanks meant a lot to me and my trip to their house had initiated another mission I now felt I had to complete…, but not until after I had seen Joel.

Chapter 20

Drowning In Self-Pity

Visiting the hospital was a nerve-wracking experience, which started well before I had even entered the building. I wasn't sure what I was expecting to find when I got there, but I felt a bout of unease. This feeling hung over me like a cloud about to burst.

My first sighting of Joel was tentative and akin to meeting somebody for the first time on a blind date. The pile of magazines, chocolates and clothes I was carrying did nothing to inspire my confidence in hoping to greet a receptive Joel. The sight of small headphones poking out from his ears quickly explained his initial ignorance of my presence. When he realised I was there he quickly threw out his arms and greeted me in a manner I did not deserve, "Am I glad to *see* you!" He laughed, "Did you see what I did there… Oops, I did it again… See… Get it? *See…*"

I nodded at his inane sense of humour, "Yes Joel, I get it."

Then he frowned, "Okay, let's hear it. Why so long?"

Knowing how he had come to be here, I found myself lying again, "Oh, nothing really. I don't really have an excuse but I am sorry and will never do it again."

This time his laugh was hesitant, "Again? I hope coming to hospital, *again,* will never happen again! There, I did it again… See!" Joel was, indeed, back on track and more like the Joel of past.

We continued our banter for a while, but I knew we both wanted to say something about the more recent past. There was no way I was going to bring up what had been going on at the cottage and beyond, so I made small talk for most of my visit, "Oh, by the way, I never did thank you for the doll's house." He looked at me quizzically before a nurse interrupted us when she came in to take his blood pressure and temperature.

By the time the nurse had gone, the subject of the doll's house had been forgotten, as Joel told me about a doctor he had taken a particular fancy to. Between the two of them, they had discussed the doctor's upcoming wedding, with Joel offering tips on dress code. The look and gesture Joel gave me made me giggle. He finished by saying that his attraction to the doctor was just pure fantasy on his part.

Eventually, I broached the subject about his reluctance to go back to the cottage, "Suzy tells me you don't want to come back to the cottage with me, is that right?"

He frowned and put away the CD player he had in his hands before replying, "It's not that I don't want to or that I don't want to be with you… but… Well, you see…, it is the house itself. I don't think she wants me to be there and, in truth, I fear for either my sanity or my life."

The question needed to be asked, "What are you talking about?" I exclaimed. Although his explanation was simple, my asking the last question was irrelevant due to my understanding of the situation. Despite this, I still felt a little aggrieved.

Joel looked at me sympathetically, "You're not compassionate like me. You wouldn't understand, but there are things about that house I defy anybody to cope with. You see, there is something about the place I cannot get my head around. Maybe… just maybe, due to my sensitive nature, I understand more than you."

I don't know why but I snapped at him before apologising, "Maybe, just maybe..." I mirrored, "This has more to do with your recent illness than anything else. Look, I'm sorry... It's just that... Oh, I don't know any more."

He grinned from ear to ear, pleased in the knowledge that I had just proved his point, "There you go... completely insensitive! You are, without doubt, completely impervious to my feelings. Look girl, there is definitely something going on there and I don't want to be part of it. Anyhow, there are things I should be doing elsewhere!" Joel felt for my hand, "Hey, I still love you with a passion, and there is nothing on this planet that will take that away. Look, I have to be honest with you and have to say that your house gives me the 'Willies'. Apart from that, I know what has happened to me and I also know my illness has nothing to do with the feelings I have about Rose Cottage."

Joel was treating me with more respect than I deserved considering my apparent lack of care and consideration toward him. I don't know why I had ignored his plight since being involved with Rose Cottage, but I guess he had a point about my lack of compassion. This might well have had something to do with the very concerns he was talking about.

We agreed that I would leave him in peace, and since I still had his car, would return when he was due for discharge. In the meanwhile, I had things to do, which included getting myself a new car since I would be isolated without one.

My choice of car and the execution of purchase amazed me and the salesman involved. After some fervent activity at the local bank, the garage delivered my nearly new Renault Clio the following week. The ex-demo model in bright red suited my needs and looked great parked outside the cottage.

Excitedly, in between all of these events, the new hinges were collected and subsequently attached to the back door by one of Noah's most trusted employees, Tom. It was good to know that Noah was on the mend but my attention was more drawn to the sight of the hinges being fitted. Nothing seemed to matter as much to me as that did! Curiously, after Tom had left, I stood and stared at the door for ages. Occasionally, I would open and close it on a whim. The net result made me feel satisfied, although for some unknown reason there were alarm bells 'going off' in my head. Surely now, with the house complete, I could now relax since the door that had meant so much to me was now whole again.

Eventually, Joel and I came to an agreement about how and when he was to be collected from the hospital. He remained adamant that he would not return to the cottage... No matter what! He also understood the complexities of me driving him back to London, and suggested he was well enough to do this by himself. After a short argument about the matter, we said our 'goodbyes' at the end of the lane and well out of sight of my home.

The walk home was cold due to an unexpected increase in the wind, which suddenly came down from the northern fields. With the winds, came a slight drizzle that seemed to cling to my clothes. By the time I got home, I was both numb and wet. The warmth of the lounge was a haven away from the weather, which appeared to come from nowhere. The rain, now heavy, beat at the windowpanes, while the wind howled through any slight gap it could find. It was this, the wind, which disturbed me the most because I swear I could hear voices from within.

Once dried, I snuggled down on the sofa and started to read, but my concentration was broken by a loud bang. I reacted quickly to discover that the back door was wide open. It had been forced back against the wall by the might of the baying winds. It took all of my strength to close the door. It wasn't until I reached the last few centimetres that I noticed something on the other side of the stream. With my body wedged tightly against the door, I looked through the horizontal rain to see something glinting in the dullness. The rain was so fierce that I had to protect my eyes from its sting. With a certain amount of effort, I closed the door and headed for the bedroom where I knew I would be able to see more.

From my vantage point, I saw something that sickened me to the core. The sight of three old ladies standing over the body of a newly sacrificed goat was enhanced by the faint glow of a lantern. Remarkably, the ladies did not seem to be affected by the weather and their demeanour was more in keeping with clement weather. Of all the things that had recently happened, this was the most significant, since it suddenly brought home the brief story Crinchley had told me of three witches.

That area surrounding the bench definitely had an important role to play in the events in and around the cottage.

There was a sudden and unexpected squall, which all but obliterated the sight before me. By the time it passed there was nothing to see other than a flattened area of meadow and mud.

I now remembered what else I had wanted to do since I visited Robin and Liz. For now though, it would have to wait.

My night was filled with all sorts of horrors, but mostly I stayed awake and listened to a series of echoes and other strange noises. I suppose the most significant and frightening of these were the much more subtle sounds. These noises appeared to be coming from within the room and from within the loft space above me. The sounds were of scraping, scratching, rustling and occasionally a series of footsteps. When I first heard the footsteps, they consisted of short light steps…, that of a child. Latter steps were clearly adult. It was only now that I unconsciously grabbed for the necklace I was no longer wearing. I did however, gain some form of comfort when I realised I still had the bracelet. Somehow, the bracelet settled so well on my wrist that I had actually forgotten it was there. With the renewed knowledge of its existence came a warmth of reassurance. I eventually drifted off into sleep.

At sunrise, I quickly showered, knowing I would soon need another. The night's events were now put to the back of my mind. During my short sleep, the rain had stopped and the wind had calmed, bringing peace to the area. With clear skies, I ventured out and soon found the spade I sought.

It didn't take long for me to dig a sizable hole in the area closest to the bench. After about an hour of digging, I came up with nothing. I then ventured to the right and at the foot of the bench. Here, I was shocked to find a collection of bones. Some of the browned bones were quite substantial in size. Although I was not certain, I was convinced they were not human. The only part of the skeleton I could not find was the skull and its absence deprived me of the knowledge I needed to identify the beast.

By the time I had finished digging, I had covered a vast area to the depth of no more than a metre. Unexpectedly, the hole then started to fill up with water from the stream. The stream's water seemed to pour in as if in an effort to cover what I had found. At first, I ignored this until the water level reached the top of my wellington boots. Because I found it difficult to climb out, I reached for the bench to support my weight. No matter how hard I tried, I couldn't…, and then it happened.

Within seconds, I found myself fighting to get out of the shallow hole but it felt like I was being held down by the ankles. The more I struggled the further I sank, until I was up to my neck in murky water. There was a sharp tugging from below and I went right under before I could grab a final breath. Frantically, and with the full weight of my body behind it, I threw my left hand upwards, grabbing at the air…, but what I felt was a hand.

The unseen but powerful grip pulled me to the surface, where I coughed and spluttered whilst gasping for the air I so desperately needed. I leaned forward and wretched in an effort to rid my lungs of the foul tasting water. My hands instinctively went to my eyes to clear my vision, as I tilted my head left and right to get sludge out from of my ears.

In the distance, I could hear a voice…, a man's voice. I called out in desperation, "Dad…, Dad, is that you? Dad, please answer me!"

The voice came back through a haze of sound and activity, "No, it's me! Edward…, Edward Crinchley. What on earth…?" His voice trailed off into the distance as I started to mutter uncontrollably.

I soon realised there wasn't enough water in the ditch for me to be submerged to the degree I felt I had. Despite this, I knew I had been in danger of drowning. With Crinchley's help, I returned to the cottage where, without thought or consideration, I stripped off naked. Like a true gentleman, he diverted his eyes as I left and ran upstairs to the shower. As I stood under the shower, I cried before stooping and cradling my arms around my body. Through my bleary eyes, I saw the dirty water run down the drain in circles. This sight seemed to mirror my own emotive thoughts. With the warmth now fully restored to my limbs and body, I dried myself and sat on the toilet seat deep in contemplation. It was then I realised what I had done in front of Crinchley and blushed. Never before had I stripped off so openly in front of anybody... save a few boyfriends from long, long ago.

It was a good hour before I re-emerged. Feeling refreshed, I went downstairs wearing my most comfortable pyjamas, and the thickest dressing gown

I owned. I wasn't sure whether Crinchley would still be there or not. I walked into the kitchen to find him sitting at my small table. He was studying the doll's house and told me I had done a wonderful job in recreating the interior. My mind was elsewhere as I scanned the room quickly in search of my dirty clothing but could see nothing out of the ordinary. Remarkably, all of my things were in the washing machine, which was contently whirring away in the background. This caused me, once more, to flush with embarrassment.

There was an awkward silence before I apologised for my actions. I quickly joked, "I am getting pretty fed up of getting wet you know!" My reference only had a slight significance to the man before me.

He partly looked my way and I could see a faint smile, "I think this has to be the most exciting thing to happen to me since my house burnt down." His laugh appeared to be more out of relief than anything else. He added quite solemnly, "It was a goat."

My brain was somewhat disconnected to the latter subject, "A goat! What on earth are you talking about?" I heard myself ask.

Crinchley stood up and walked to the window. He appeared to be looking towards the bench, "The bones you found were that of a goat. I know my livestock and that was definitely a goat." I questioned how he had seen it in all of the muck, and his answer was simple, "You left the most significant of the bones on the bench." It was true I had, but the blurriness of the situation had made me lose all concept of reality during my ordeal.

Only now did I think to thank Crinchley for saving my life, "Thank you! Thank you for saving me. Oh, and thank you for not minding about…, you know…" I coyly looked down. He knew what I was thanking him for and his reaction proved my sense of ease in his presence. He bowed his head in a shallow nod without saying a word.

I chirped up once more, "Cuppa?"

Between us, we had a renewed understanding as he once more nodded. With the kettle on, I started to make the tea when I realised the sugar bowl was empty.

The larder was as it should be and filled to capacity with goodies and other essentials. The bag of sugar was perched high on the shelf and almost out of my reach. I considered calling for Crinchley's help but felt foolish under the circumstances. With full determination, I tipped the bag towards me and was shocked when it crashed down upon my head and finally hit the floor where it burst open. I picked up what little remained in the bag before swearing at the mess around my feet. "Shit!" I muttered. 'That can wait until later' I thought.

We drank our tea and ate the biscuits I specifically kept for comfort moments like this.

Crinchley asked me a question that must have been at the forefront of his mind, "Can you please explain what was going on when I found you? And what the hell were you digging for?" His beautiful voice once again soothed me.

My answer was simple but chilling, "Julianne." I replied.

Chapter 21

Foundations

My explanation to Crinchley of recent events fell short since I failed to mention the vision prior to my digging venture. The thought of the three women caused a chill to rush over my body, and the sight of the poor sacrificial goat gave me goose bumps. With Crinchley confirming the identity of the animal bones, I felt almost too scared to repeat what I saw. It was almost as, by mentioning it again, I would evoke some sort of realism to it all.

The logic I used to identify the area as a shallow grave was purely based on the vision I had seen in the recent deluge. Couple this with the previous night's events I had felt compelled to achieve something - but had effectively failed miserably. The necklace also featured in my reckoning since that is where I 'found' it, or perhaps more accurately, where it found me. Surely, I tried to convince myself, based on these points, the connections were far too strong for me to ignore.

I now had a fatalistic view about my reasons for being here at Rose Cottage. Everything that had happened up until now was meant to be. The very reason I was here at all, had more to do with forces beyond my comprehension than for any other reason. So, my newfound outlook based on recent events now seemed valid. It was either that or my sanity was now in question.

Edward Crinchley left later that day with some reassuring words, "Look... Claire, if there is anything you need or if something is bothering you, then peg a white handkerchief from the upstairs back window. I am around a lot more than you think..." He faltered slightly, "You see I often tend to the woods and am always in the vicinity. You do understand that your welfare is my first thought? Right?"

I looked at him and nodded with a smile whilst trying to remain calm. For the first time since we had met, he seemed at total ease in my presence. He no longer hid his face or right hand from my view, and no longer seemed to worry about speaking so openly.

The evening and night passed quickly and I slept remarkably well considering my most recent ordeal. There were no bad dreams or 'bumps in the night' to cause me any concern, so the bright morning light was a welcome sight for all of the right reasons. My intention was to go outside and fill in the hole to make safe a potential hazard. To my utmost amazement, I looked out of my window to see Crinchley walking away from a neatly covered area next to the bench. Gone too were the pile of bones that I had left on the bench. I felt foolish knowing what I had done and now, in the cold light of the day, realised I must have slipped when I was in the hole before panicking. Being disorientated, I must have lain down and imagined I was sinking downwards and not, as I was, lying across the pond I had created. Sure, who wouldn't react like that after the trauma I had endured up until then? I thought back and added all of the occurrences together since I had arrived here, and tried to put a logical spin on things. In truth, there were far too many for me to explain properly but I desperately wanted to believe there were rational grounds for their happenings. I even considered the fact that I was hallucinating due to some form of gas leakage. It brought to mind the story of 'The Pythia', the Priestess of Delphi and her purported stimulation brought on by inhaling ethylene gas. I laughed at the thought and the absurd correlation.

I now needed the strange events to stop for me to completely believe this, but it was about to become much worse… much, much worse!

I sat down for my morning coffee full of confidence and, to a degree, optimism. I slowly sipped my drink and realised that I had either not sugared it or not stirred it, whichever - it tasted bitter. As I stirred my coffee, I spied the sugar bowl, which reminded me that I had a mess to clear up in the larder.

Since I no longer had a hole to fill in the garden, I decided to start the day with some specific chores. I even thought about doing something I had neglected for longer than I cared to think about. By this, I mean that I appeared to have forgotten about my computer and the joys it had once brought me. For some strange reason, up and until now, I no longer felt the need to use it as much as I once did. In fact, my neglect went well beyond all reason, since the computer used to be my whole life. One sure fire way of me forgetting about recent events would perhaps be to resurrect my avatar 'Finitia'. As 'Finitia', I could do almost anything, from fighting ogres in forests to dragons in castles and even witches in dungeons. Yes. Why not I thought.

After my chores, I was going to fight battles I knew I could win.

The sun continued to shine as I bounced down the stairs full of vigour. My cleaning cupboard was the least used of all the storerooms, but I didn't care. Amongst my cleaning products were a series of power tools and extension cables left behind by the builders in their haste to leave. On several occasions, I called their offices to invite them back to collect them as they were cluttering up my space, but to no avail.

Putting the appliances to one side, I found what I was looking for.

With dustpan and brush in hand I headed for the larder door, although, I was soon stopped in my tracks by a familiar sound. I answered my mobile to hear the chirpy voice of Joel, "Hey Girl! Hope you are well. Look, I need you up here tomorrow and I shall not take no as an answer." I cautiously questioned both his motives and the urgency. He simply said, "Par-tay!" There was no real reason for me to ignore his request and since I still felt so guilty about my past shabbiness toward him, I readily agreed. Frankly, his parties were the talk of the town and it would be good to get away for a short break. We agreed I would be there by noon, which seemed to please Joel no end.

The larder door stuck briefly as I tugged at it, before it opened with a lurch. I looked down and was surprised by the complete lack of mess on the floor. What was once a pile of sugar had turned out to be nothing more than a few scattered granules. At first, I suspected mice as the reason for the loss of sugar. I shrugged and stooped down to sweep up these last few granules and started by piling them together. As I did so, most of the small grains slipped down through the cracks of the worn stone floor and out of sight. It was not as if they fell into the shallow crevices between the stones but disappeared out of sight into a hollow beneath!

Due to curiosity, I quickly sought out a torch and headed back to the larder. I peered through the gaps and concluded that there must be a space below the floor on which I was now kneeling. To prove this point I gathered two items and went to experiment. The remaining sugar from the bowl was conclusive as far as the hollowness was concerned and the penny confirmed depth as I heard a muffled thud when it hit the bottom. Excitedly, I went outside and grabbed the recently well-used spade to use as a lever. With the cutting edge of the spade fully inserted, I pushed down hard and tilted its handle towards me. This, in turn, caused a loud creaking sound so I paused fearful that the handle would break. I knew the amount of strain I was exerting on the spade would cause a real problem if it were to break, but I persevered. Moments later, the flagstone eased up with a grating noise before I heard a subtle pop. This noise confirmed success. Gently, I eased the heavy stone to one side and propped it up against the larder wall. The hole under the stone revealed what looked like a now defunct cellar.

Of course, the opening was far too small for me to wriggle down, however, it was just enough for me to get my head and one shoulder through. As I did so, I became aware of a musty smell that reminded me of damp mushroom compost. With a great deal of dexterity, I managed to swing my arm down into the space. In my eagerness to survey the area, I fumbled and dropped the torch, which fell out of reach. The torch hit something solid and rolled around in circles for a while before coming to a stop hard against a wall like structure. Frustratingly, the torch light was facing the wrong way and even further out of reach.

For a while, I sat on my haunches and considered my next move. Logic stated that I should wait and get assistance from Crinchley, but impulsiveness took over. Carefully, I managed to prise another flagstone away from its setting. Now that the space had been opened up, I managed to crawl down and into the now cavernous space. The torch, uncharacteristically flickered as I picked it up, which denoted a problem. It was soon obvious there was something wrong with the glass. A closer inspection proved that the glass had indeed cracked in two places. Although not completely useless, the fractured glass threw a strange arc like shadow as it projected deep into the dark.

I now felt very, very much alone!

Chapter 22

Confrontation

In essence, what I had found was a separate building. A building within another if you will.

From where I stood, I could just about see steps leading upwards, which if my geography was right, would lead into the garden. There were several cupboards, a bookshelf with two books upon it, a rocking chair, a doll, a small oven and two empty picture frames. At the furthest end of the bookshelf, was an eclectic mix of crockery and something that resembled an oil lamp. The lamp looked very similar to the one I had seen in my vision of the three old ladies. At the base of one of the picture frames, was a single picture of three women standing aside a man and flanked by a black cat. I could only make out two of the faces since the third and fourth, the man, had been obscured by mould. The man stood tall and seemed to be wearing a hat of sorts.

I backed up as I heard a sound from above and made my way to the opening, only to hear a further sound of what appeared to be a man grunting. Within moments, the flagstones had been replaced, leaving me trapped in the depths of my own house! I screamed to let the person know that I was down there but they ignored my shouts. The opening was the only other source of light and this rapidly disappeared as something heavy was dragged over the two replaced flagstones. It was obvious that somebody had deliberately incarcerated me, but what were their intentions? Whoever they were, they were immediately unknown to me.

Why would anybody do such a thing?

Anxiously, I stood directly underneath the flagstones. My heart was pounding as I peered upwards to see what was blocking the flagstones. Using the waning power of the torch, I could only see the darkness but soon focused on what looked like wood. What was on top of that, I could only guess. Something crunched underfoot and I looked down at a small pile of sugar when a strange thought hit me. Whether I was joking to keep my spirits up or whether it was out of hopelessness, I heard myself saying, "Best save that. It might be my last meal." And in truth hopelessness was what I now felt. I was trapped under my own house where nobody would ever find me.

I shivered at the prospect and felt that now familiar panic.

Self-preservation then cut in and I ran to the cupboard to see what I could find that would help me with… *To help with what?* I questioned.

Apart from dust, I found very little before having an idea. I smashed a china plate from the shelf and picked up the largest of the pieces. With sheer determination, I started to gouge into the earth high at the end of the furthest wall. This section of wall was the only section not constructed of brick. My logic was to dig myself out and into the garden above.

At first, the soil came away easily…, a little too easily. The wall then started to collapse, seconds before water started to seep in. "Water? No! No!" I jumped backwards to avoid getting wet, and collided with the rocking chair. The impact sent the doll skywards. For its size, it landed softly as I ventured further back and away from the spreading water.

I now knew exactly where I was in conjunction to the lay of the land. I was near or directly below the stream! I was going to drown!

With no options left open to me, I ran back to the opening where I had initially entered. Although blocked, I sought to try to use my strength and pushed upwards on the underside of the floor. With any luck, I would be able to dislodge whatever was on top of the flagstone. I pushed hard, causing nothing more than subtle movements. Occasionally, stray grains of sugar that were embedded in the flagstones above showered me. And then the inevitable happened, as I found myself temporarily blinded as a particle or two entered my eye.

Scared and angry, I cursed out aloud, "Fuck! Fuck!"

No longer was the sugar beneath my feet making a crunching sound, since the water was now up to my ankles. Using my sleeve, I managed to wipe away the tears from my watering eye before continuing what I had started. My height wasn't sufficient enough, so I went back to get the rocking chair. With more than a little effort, I managed to break off the rockers. I did this so I could find purchase when standing upon it, without the fear falling off. With all my strength, I pushed upwards using my shoulders and back - which did little - although there was some movement. I knew that if at each stage of pushing, I could stop the flagstone from coming back down then I might get somewhere. At first, I used the two detached rockers as levers but they snapped easily. The broken pieces served well as stops, which allowed me to form a gap between the larder floor and the flagstone I was so desperately pushing.

This gave me hope.

I worked relentlessly at trying to force the gap wider, but after what seemed an age I had only managed to open up a gap of no more than twenty centimetres or so. Exhausted I gave one more final push, which then created a situation I would have rather not have faced as the chair broke, causing me to fall into the rising water. With a look of desperation, I splashed and screamed for all I was worth. Ironically, my thoughts went back to the conversation I had just had with Crinchley about getting wet.

This time though the thought neither inspired me, nor amused me - it just terrified me.

The rippling effect I had just caused made something bump up against me. As I turned my rapidly fading torch toward the item, I screamed even louder than I had before.

Impulsively, I clamped my hand to my mouth to stifle another scream as I found myself staring directly into the blackened face of a mummified Julianne Alsford!

The doll I had so recklessly dismissed was none other than the girl in my dreams. Her clothes should have told me this earlier but I was too engrossed in getting out of the enforced prison I found myself. She looked so small… So tiny compared to the girl in my visions.

In a delayed reaction, I clambered backwards and fell deeper into the water, which now seemed to be rising more quickly.

Julianne's body now appeared to be bobbing upright. It was almost as if her feet were tethered to the floor. Her eyeless gaze followed me as I thrashed about in the muddy water. Desperately, I tried not to look at her but found that impossible since there was a part of me that needed to. It was now that I noticed the trauma to her head and neck area. Although I couldn't be certain due to the amount of decomposition, I would say that she had had her throat cut.

My resolve was diminishing. I just knew I was going to die down here alongside her. Whether we would be found was a reality I tried not to think about too deeply. I screamed out once more just before the torch faded completely.

With a faint glimmer of hope, I suddenly remembered my phone and felt for it. I found it and pulled it from my back pocket. Immediately, I placed it to my ear, only to find that the water had penetrated the phone's plastic cover. There was no way I was going to be able to use it now. Not even if

I found a signal, which I then had to admit was highly unlikely.

With the water now at chest height, I felt certain in the knowledge Julianne and I were about to share the same tomb.

Chapter 23

Mending Bridges

With my fate as good as sealed, I suddenly became calm and thought of my parents and Nanny Rose. My parents' faces were as clear to me now as they ever were when they were alive. Strangely though, Nanny's face was cloudy and dull, which seemed to me sad and unexplained. But then it seemed, nothing about my situation had an explanation.

As I contemplated my impending death I heard a noise above. I screamed with all my might to draw attention to myself. Soon after this, I heard a scraping noise; similar to what I had heard earlier when I first became entombed.

With the first crack of light, I called out with ever-increasing urgency, "Hello… Please help me… Help me… I'm here… Down here!"

At first, the bright light from above temporarily blinded me and all I could see was a series of shadows. Seconds later, and much to my relief, the second flagstone was removed. Within minutes, I was being forcibly pulled upwards and out of the cellar. At first, I was relieved to see my rescuer, and then I began to have doubts. The shock was making my head spin.

Crinchley looked concerned and started to ask all sorts of questions, "What on earth are you doing? How in hell's name, did you become trapped down there? What…?"

I stopped him from asking any more questions with several of my own, "Did you do this to me? My so-called hero. Always near enough to save the day? But why? What is going on…? Is this what you do?"

Despite his disfigurement, I could see a certain amount of horror and hurt on his face. My aggressive attitude made me sound and feel like a demented woman.

Crinchley turned and side stepped the doll's house, which must have been the obstruction I tried so hard to shift. Within seconds, I was left alone, not quite knowing what to do. One minute I feared my worst nightmare, and the next I was being rescued only to accuse my saviour of entombing me in the first place.

Soaking wet, I ran after him shouting. Eventually, I caught up just as he crossed the stream. It was clear that he was upset and before I could apologise he turned and pointed to something over my shoulder. I looked behind to see exactly where he was pointing. When I saw it, the sight made me quiver. There, as clear as day, was a white handkerchief pegged to the curtain inside the bedroom window.

Crinchley once more turned and started to walk away but I held his arm firmly, "I am sorry… So, very, very sorry!" I cried before falling to my knees. He stopped and turned to face me but had by now, resumed the defensive posture he had used before we got to know each other. By covering his scars, he was telling me that he had lost trust in me… and who could blame him. I pleaded with him to stop, "Please stop… Don't go… I've found Julianne!"

In an instant, he returned to my side and dropped to his knees to face me. He placed his hands upon my shoulders, "What!?" He almost shouted.

I pointed toward the house and begged him to come back with me, "She was down there with me… I thought I was going to die."

For the first time ever, he pulled me towards him and hugged me tightly. As soon as he let me go, he lowered his head to reach my eye line and stared into my eyes, "Is it true? Have you really found her?"

I merely nodded.

I was far too traumatised to question the 'how's and why's' of the appearance of the white handkerchief, and Crinchley never mentioned it either since we now had other things on our minds.

We both ran back to the cottage and I apologised every step of the way. No matter how many times he accepted my apology I added another. Crinchley seemed like a man possessed and continued as if he was on an urgent mission. Before I crossed the river, I roughly calculated the distance I was away from the larder. By doing this, I established where I was in conjunction to my place of captivity. I could then see a series of bubbles coming from the far side of the stream and knew exactly where the water was entering the cellar.

When I reached the larder, I stopped short of entering and tentatively pushed Crinchley ahead of me. He stopped in his tracks just outside the larder then without thought, dropped into the exposed cavity.

It didn't take long for Crinchley to locate Julianne's body and when he did, he wept like no other man I had seen before. Somehow, I just knew he was actually weeping for his lost daughter and wife. I also knew that those who still suspected he had a role to play in Julianne's disappearance would finally vindicate him. From now on, all eyes would now be focused on Rose Cottage, Mabel Adams… and I suppose, to a degree, me too.

It wasn't long before the police and fire services arrived in their droves.

The senior police officer was, at a guess, close to retiring. My initial assumption was proved right as he almost confirmed this point on introduction, "Hello Miss Chambers, how are you coping after your ordeal?" Wrapped in a blanket, I explained my version of events before he added, "Oh, how remiss of me. I am DI Graham Hockley, Wiltshire Police. Let me get straight to the point. For me personally, Miss Julianne Alsford is quite an important case. It was one of the first cases to come my way when I became involved with C.I.D. I was never entirely satisfied with the overall outcome of our original enquiries, but with workloads as they were then… Well, I had to move on. I am due to retire soon and this, of all the cases I have ever handled, was the one I most wanted to solve. Unfortunately, the water damage has all but destroyed any evidence that might have been down there but at least we… Sorry, you…, will have given Liz and Robin some form of closure."

DI Hockley had a way of making me feel at ease, and his slight West Country accent lulled me into believing everything was now going to be all right.

Before we could continue we were approached by a fire fighter, "We've shored up the wall at the far end of the cellar and also sunk trench sheets into the stream. There is no way the water will ever come through there again. By the way, we have finished pumping out the water and have filtered the mud, just as you had asked. Oh, another thing Miss, we had some spare boards with us so we have placed them across the stream for your future safety." He gave a half salute to DI Hockley and a beaming smile to me before running back towards the house.

DI Hockley held me by my elbow and gently led me towards the house. As we walked, he continued by asking me a searching question, "What do you know of Mr Crinchley?"

After my accusations toward Crinchley and Crinchley's understandable reactions to them, I knew he had nothing to do with my captivity. In light of this, I countered accordingly, "I do hope you are not suggesting that he had anything to do with this." My answer was intensified with all the indignity I could muster.

There was a surprised look on DI Hockley's face, "Oh no! Good grief! No! In fact, it was me who cleared him at the time I investigated his alibi. No, what I meant was do you know of his background? The only reason I ask, is because I need you to know certain things. By me mentioning this now, I hope you will have no prejudices later when you find out what I have to say. You see, he has had a lot to cope with over the years and I don't want him upset any more than needs be..."

I rudely interrupted DI Hockley before telling him that I knew of Crinchley's background and trusted him implicitly. It wasn't long before I was asked another question, "Okay then, answer me this. Who do you think placed the handkerchief in the window? Mr Crinchley has told us that he responded to a prearranged signal you had in place. Is this true?"

I searched for an answer before responding, "I don't know."

DI Hockley was quick to seize my answer, "You don't know what?"

I quickly realised my answer was insufficient and carried all sorts of implications, "Oh, sorry. I mean I don't know who put the handkerchief there and yes, we did have an arrangement in place should I need his assistance." When all was said and done, I then began to wonder who had placed it there. Surely, the person who had entrapped me wouldn't have done that. Although, how would anybody else know of our arrangement? To my knowledge, only Crinchley and I knew of this plan.

DI Hockley then led me into the house where he passed me over to a WPC who was there specifically to take my statement. Before he left, DI Hockley had one more thing to tell me, "Don't worry about the handkerchief. We have taken it and the peg away for analysis. We shall work it out in due course."

I thanked him before making a full statement to WPC Bailey.

Following my report, I looked for Crinchley who was sitting in a quiet corner of my garden. He was as damp as I was and looked at me in a pitiful sort of way before merely nodding in my general direction as I approached. Now that we had both given our version of events, we spoke of the ordeal. By the time we had finished the discussions, we had established a new and better understanding of each other. He told me he was so relieved that Julianne had finally been found and that it had also brought to an end a personal struggle. His only wish was that we could remain friends to which there could only be one answer… Yes. He then suggested I book into a hotel for a night or two while the police 'did what they had to do'. For some unknown reason I asked if he had room at his place because I didn't want to leave the immediate area.

He looked at me in confusion, "I'm not sure that is such a good idea. I mean what will people say and…"

I took his right hand and felt the smoothness of his skin and the contrasting contours of the scars caused by the burns, "To be quite honest, I don't care what people say or think. You and I both know that there is nothing but friendship between us. So frankly, they can all go to hell. Apart from that I would feel safer in your company than anywhere else at this moment."

Crinchley dropped his shoulders and smiled, as I have never seen before.

Chapter 24

Blood Ties

Before we went back to Crinchley's barn, we both paid a visit to the Alsford's to offer our condolences. This visit was at my behest and no matter what; I was not going to accept no as an answer. Crinchley admitted he didn't feel comfortable about doing this but I forced the issue further, "Look, we both need some form of closure here, perhaps you more so than me. Maybe this will help both of us."

He nodded, perhaps to keep the peace more than for any other reason.

Crinchley stood behind me as I knocked purposefully on the door. There was quite a pause before the door was answered, and even then, it only opened tentatively. Robin peered out, "Oh, it's you. Sorry, I thought you were some more reporters. Liz told me that if it were them…" He immediately stopped speaking when he realised I was not alone before adding, "Oh. Edward."

There was another moment of pause before he spoke again, "I'm sorry, where are my manners? Please, please come in." He looked at Crinchley and seemed lost for words, "Oh, I wasn't expecting… Can I take your coats…?" There was another pause as he looked us both up and down, "My, you're both wet. Look… Come in and I'll get some towels." He left us for a moment before returning with a confused look on his face, "Now where was I going…, Oh, yes…"

Was this really the same man I had once sat opposite, and felt the full vigour of his glare? Here before me was a much more subservient man… A man in total disarray.

With towels in hand, Robin took us through to the hub of the house and announced our arrival, "Liz, we have guests. It's Edward and Claire. Can you believe it? They're both here…, together."

I found it quite telling that Crinchley had been introduced before me.

For a while, Liz stared at Crinchley before telling him that she was sorry that he had gone through so much due to her daughter's disappearance. Crinchley almost immediately dismissed her apology as not being necessary since he had no problem with them. He knew, unlike so many others, that they publically condemned what had happened to him. Robin, on the other hand, seemed speechless knowing that the man accused of having an input in the disappearance of his daughter was standing in his house. Then, all of a sudden, it was as if Robin was struck by an invisible force, "Tea… yes. We must all have tea." He started to prepare a brew as if his life depended upon it before suddenly breaking down, "Julianne…, Julianne…, Edward…, I am so sorry! I let you both down, and then did nothing to stop you from being punished for something you did not do…"

He sobbed openly as Liz went to his side and held him affectionately.

I now felt guilty for the intrusion and I think Crinchley would have preferred to be anywhere else other than here, "Look, Robin…, Liz… You were not to blame for what happened to me, besides, I'm here because… Well, because…" Crinchley looked at me before finishing his sentence, "Well, I'm here because I too want to say sorry…"

Robin looked up with his tearful eyes and looked at Crinchley, "Sorry. Edward, we have lost a daughter - but you found her for us. I only wish we could have done something for you when you most needed our help. We all loved your Cathy and young

Fiona…" What was said next shocked me to the core, "…our beloved niece. When you married Cathy, we couldn't have been happier and we know the accident was… Well, just that, an accident. It wasn't your fault."

Crinchley sat down as I looked from person to person without quite understanding the full picture that had just unfolded before me. Liz then walked over to Crinchley and knelt before him, "Edward, my brother… I have… that is we have…" She looked back toward Robin before continuing, "…always loved you, but after the fire you wouldn't let us anywhere near you. I suppose, following Cathy and Fiona, this was your worst nightmare. Please believe me when I say that we knew you had nothing to do with what happened to Julianne." She looked back toward Robin again as Crinchley now sobbed.

A picture had now fully formed itself in my head, "So you're brother and sister then!" I exclaimed. Up until the moment I spoke, I had been in blissful isolation, since between them I had all but been forgotten.

I too, sat down.

Crinchley pulled himself together and looked at me sideways, "I'm sorry Claire, I should have told you but I didn't know how to."

For a long while after this overwhelming revelation, we all sat in silence as each of us absorbed the importance of this meeting. It was obvious to everybody, except me, that this discussion would have eventually come about, but Crinchley said nothing until now. He didn't object to coming to the house, so I suspect either he didn't want to let me down or, more importantly, he needed to come here. I concluded that by finding Julianne, he had also decided to face his own demons.

Crinchley and I told them everything we knew. There were more tears and just as many questions, mostly from Robin and Liz, and mostly aimed at me. However, one very important question was on all of our minds. It was Liz who asked, "Who do you think sealed you in the cellar?"

The last question DI Hockley had asked me had finally come up and, once again, I came up with a blank. I thought long and hard before answering, "The police asked me the same question and I really don't have an answer." To be honest, I hadn't made a connection to anybody in particular and couldn't think of another solitary person since I had eliminated Crinchley.

Then I asked the one question I had pondered for ages, "Who is Marcie?"

My question was met by a sea of blank faces before Liz spoke, "Never heard of her. Why?" I then went on to explain what I had, or thought I had seen in my kitchen, "The cat seemed real to me. The smell and the infestation of flies were real enough. Oh, I don't know, perhaps this was all my imagination." I wanted to finish on a positive note so I added, "The important thing is that we found Julianne."

Crinchley was the next to speak, "Perhaps you may recall what I said about the cat being found in the original house. Legend has it that it came back to life and perhaps you dreamt about that after I told you."

I frowned before admitting that this event happened *before* he told me the story, "Oh, I don't know, but Marcie was definitely the name I saw written on the floor. Does anybody know the names of the witches who lived at Rose Cottage? Perhaps she was one of them."

There was silence. Just silence.

There were clearly no answers to my question so I dropped the subject, since it now seemed too macabre, especially under the circumstances.

It was only now, Liz realised why we had damp towels in our hands and suggested to Robin that he found an assortment of clothes for us to change into. Crinchley refused a change of clothing, whereas I donned a mix of outer clothes. I assumed they were Liz's, so I planned to have them cleaned and returned at the earliest moment.

The rest of the day was filled with positive thoughts and discussions, although I never really understood one particular point that was generally muted. Both Liz and Robin, and to a certain degree, Crinchley, seemed to believe that Julianne would eventually be found dead. None of them appeared to have held onto the hope that Julianne may have been abducted and be living somewhere else. For now though, their emotions seemed to centre on the fact that her body had now been found and they could now bury her in peace.

I suppose, I couldn't quite grasp the thought that, to them, this was now all over.

Chapter 25

Dark Dreams

The evening was cold and the distant moonlight gave the panoramic view a mystical look.

As we walked back to Crinchley's barn, I asked him how he felt about the most recent of events. His answer was quite telling, "I'm relieved really. There were times when I thought I should have seen Robin and Liz sooner. Today turned out to be the right thing to do. Perhaps now, there will be peace in all of our hearts. For that, I thank you."

From a distance, we could clearly see the cottage. The temporary arc lights fitted by the police, made the scene look surreal as my home was bathed in a light I don't think she liked. The reason I say this, was that the shadows thrown by the light made some areas look ominous. It was almost as if she wanted to be alone in her time of grief and hated the enforced attention.

The quickest way to Crinchley's barn was through my back garden, so we headed that way. As we approached, a uniformed policeman stopped us. No matter how much I explained, he would not let us through. I argued that I had to get a few things to see me through the night and even used DI Hockley's name to gain some credit. None of this worked, so Crinchley took me by the arm and led me an alternative route.

To get to his barn now, we needed to cross one field away from Rose Cottage. From where we stood, we could see the glow of the lights in the distance. We ventured deeper into the wooded area, which seemed to me to be alive with mystery. We did not appear to be alone. I moved closer to Crinchley as soon as I heard some faint noises ahead. Crinchley seemed to be oblivious to these noises and carried on regardless. Suddenly he stopped dead in his tracks. "Hello, what are you doing here?" I could neither see who he was talking to, nor hear a reply. As I stood firmly rooted to the ground, he ventured two steps forward and stopped once more, "Come on now, you know you shouldn't be in here… Hey, what on earth are you doing?"

I cannot properly describe how I felt about what happened next, but I was petrified and spun around in the dark to try to see what was happening. From out of the gloom came movement, and with that movement came a cry from Crinchley as he sank to his knees. He moaned slightly and was soon out of my sight as a herd of sheep - Crinchley's sheep - then surrounded me. Up until then, there was silence, as they appeared to creep up upon us before unleashing a solid wall of noise. It was as if each one of the sheep wanted to get a look at me as they circled around. Occasionally, they very carefully brushed up against me. Their touches were gentle and I soon got the impression that they meant me no harm. The noise they were making reached a sudden crescendo before utter silence. Within seconds, there was an unexpected and completely definable moment of complete quiet. Astonishingly, there was a parting of the ways as a ram ventured forward and stopped before me. His head dropped and I thought for a moment that he was going to ram me, but he didn't. He just bowed and then turned and left with his harem in close pursuit. I couldn't for the life of me work out what had just happened. I then recalled Joel's irrational fear of the sheep when they had surrounded the cars many months ago, but I didn't feel that fear. I just seem to remember that I was aware of them curiously observing me... and, like now, I wondered why.

I needed to find Crinchley, and there was just about enough moonlight for me to see where he was laying. He was doubled over in pain and struggled to get to his feet, "Crinchley!" I cried. He raised one hand before getting up on one knee. I stumbled slightly in my haste to get to his side. With great concern, I asked him if he was all right. His initial reply was laboured and thick with expletives.

For several long minutes I crouched by his side before he felt well enough to stand. He eventually spoke in short burst, "Bloody hell…! In all my years… of farming… I have never… been charged… by a ram before. What the hell… is going on?" He quickly turned to me, "Are you hurt…? I mean… did they hurt you… in any way?" I merely shook my head and smiled before he added, "Right in the… Ouch, he got me right in the…" The sentence need not be finished as, for some reason I started to laugh, and not long afterwards, Crinchley joined in.

We walked, or in Crinchley's case hobbled, a bit further in silence. Crinchley suddenly stopped and leaned forward with his hands on his knees. I asked him if he was well enough to continue or if he needed a rest. His reply was curt, "Yes…, I mean No…, Oh, bugger!" We rested for a moment longer before, once more setting off.

Within a minute or so, I saw his barn bathed in a spectacular moonlight. The sight was such that I had to stop and admire the view. As we stood absorbing the spectacle, an owl swooped down before us and plucked its prey from the nearby short grass. There was a slight squeal followed by a brief but loud cry of sudden death as the owl's talons gripped its victim ever tighter.

As we approached, I felt a presence that seemed to bypass Crinchley. I was convinced there was something silently lurking in the shadows watching our every move. Crinchley caused me to jump as he stopped, letting out a loud screeching whistle, which appeared to come from the depths of his body. From almost nowhere his two Collies sprang into action and came to their master's side. At first, they acted as if I wasn't there, unlike Arnold's dog, Maggs. This was to become my first full on meeting with them… and it was to be an everlasting relationship. Individually, they approached me and offered their right paw as a mark of friendship. I, of course, graciously accepted.

There was no electricity within the barn, which meant our only source of light came from oil lamps. Crinchley moved some makeshift furniture about and rearranged some bales of hay. With a little imagination, he had created what I would have wished for as a child. Here, I found myself in a labyrinth of comfort, as the bales represented insulated walls and a tarpaulin strung above served well as a ceiling. In an instant, I was transformed back to being a child and playing 'house' under the table at Nanny Rose's home. Tonight, the giant 'table cloth' above my head gave me the impression of parity to actual size, then and now.

My bed was a simple fold out cot with three sets of 'X' shaped legs and a remarkably new sleeping bag. My improvised bedside table was an upside down 'Watney's Red Barrel' wooden crate. Finally, and less inviting, was a shiny galvanised bucket, which was to serve as my own personal toilet. Reluctant as I was, I found it a necessity during the night. Peeing in a bucket felt and sounded strange, this in turn, caused me to giggle at the absurdity of it all. My frivolity soon turned to more serious affairs, when I noticed an eerie shadow cast itself above my head. I watched cautiously as a shadow of a cat 'walked' silently from one side of the tarpaulin to the other. The strange thing here was that between the source of the light at the foot of my bed, and the shadow cast upon the makeshift ceiling there was nothing tangible. Not even the dogs reacted to what I could see and I soon wondered if it had actually ever happened.

The long shadow eventually disappeared from view but not from my mind, as I fought to come to terms with this newfound experience. Although I was not scared, I remained cautiously alert.

This latest experience seemed trivial by comparison to what had already happened, but again I was worried.

Why now? What was going on? I could to a degree, understand Julianne's spirit needing closure. In fact, I had based my whole understanding on this. To me, by laying her body to rest, her spirit would surely rest too. So why was I still experiencing these strange occurrences?

Currently feeling the way I was, meant I was loath to put out the lamp, so I turned it to its lowest setting. I lay watching the flickering flame dance across the tarpaulin and soon drifted off into a deep sleep.

The first part of the dream I had was as bizarre as the last, which would finally bring me out of my slumber altogether. The first centred on the cat and its ability to turn into human form. The latter part had me as *Finitia,* fighting and eventually slaying an evil entity. In the dream, the cat's transformation into a human form was more frightening, since the appearance was hideous. The face I saw in my dream was indeterminate as far as sex was concerned, but I guessed it to be female. The eyes were black with no sign of whiteness and its skin was pallid, leathery and pitted. The squat nose was walnut-like with short black hair growing in tufts from several warts. 'Her' hair was as black as sin, long and straight without any sort of sheen. There was an associated smell, which lingered. The smell was like rancid butter and increased in potency the deeper I got into the dream. Before I could no longer stand the smell, I seemed to move on to the next part of the dream. This vision centred on a castle entrance where *Finitia* was forced to face a foe of extreme evil. Using her special skills, *Finitia* was able to defeat the beast but not before receiving several near fatal blows herself. With sparks flying and mutilated bodies strewn all around, *Finitia* needed every ounce of her strength and guile to survive the onslaught. This she did… but only just!

There was something very significant about the finale, although it wasn't until later, that I was able to recall its meaning. The ending started with an extreme brightness coming from the background. In fact, the light was coming from around the framework of the portcullis situated directly behind *Finitia's* foe.

In turn, the morning light was extremely welcoming. The sound and smell of frying eggs made it even more comforting.

As Crinchley and I ate our breakfast, I looked around the ramshackle barn noting the complete lack of personal effects. Everything I saw was for practical use only, and appeared to function well as a base but not as a home. This saddened me, since in the short time I had been at Rose Cottage I had done everything to make it homely.

I was about to broach this subject when there was a sudden noise coming from the entrance. The dogs became agitated but remained in situ as their master gave them a series of commands via hand signals.

Crinchley cautiously approached the door and resumed the familiar pose of cap down over his eyes. I heard hushed voices before he returned with DI Hockley in tow. Crinchley grabbed some bits and pieces before addressing me, "He's here to see you so I'll be on my way. Should you feel the need to stay longer then…" He turned and looked at the policeman before he finished speaking, then left. The dogs followed their master without a sound.

DI Hockley stood in the centre of the room and looked around much in the same way I had just done, "Not too homely is it?" Without waiting for a reply he continued, "Anyhow, I trust you had a good night and weren't too inconvenienced by what we were doing at your property. One of my officers suggested that you might be here. Sorry if he was a bit offhand, but he was only doing his job. I must say, you have done wonders with the place…, and the kitchen. Wow! You know, the last time I was there it had a presence, which I now understand. All that time, I was within reaching distance of Julianne's body and didn't even know it."

I wasn't sure what I was supposed to say, so I remained silent.

He continued, "You are free to move back into the comfort of your home..." There was a dramatic conclusion to his sentence, "...BUT, we will probably be calling back from time to time. You see, we have fresh evidence in the way of a photograph. Well, in truth it is half of a photograph, which our experts are looking into as we speak. Also, the peg holding the handkerchief hanging in the bedroom has a clear thumbprint and a partial on it."

I thought about the photograph he mentioned and asked if it was the one I had found of three women and a man. He said yes. He also added that although the photograph was damaged, the water had cleaned it up a little and that the 'techs' at the lab had the means to improve it even more. He added, "I hope that by establishing their identities, we will be able to move the case forward."

DI Hockley then leaned forward and handed me a piece of paper, "Here is a receipt for what we have taken, which by the way, includes your computer. I had heard that you have had problems with it during the past few months, so I thought I would let our experts look at it for you."

This snippet of information had me baffled, since I thought it was only Joel and I who knew of the problems.

I remained silent for a little while longer and watched DI Hockley as he looked around for somewhere to sit. He settled on a bale of hay, "I understand you went to see Mr and Mrs Alsford. That threw us a bit since we had not wanted to go and see them until we had firm evidence that the body you found was indeed their daughter. Oh, don't get me wrong… I don't blame you but would have preferred to have seen them myself." I apologised as he stood, brushed himself down and bid me, 'farewell until the next time'. As he approached the door he stopped, turned around took one last look around before making a tutting sound, then left.

Chapter 26

Sobering Thoughts

I was about to leave the barn but returned to empty the bucket to avoid the embarrassment of Crinchley having to do it. As I did so, I looked up and into the distance where I could see Crinchley with his flock. I wasn't sure but he appeared to be talking to his ram and using his arms in doing so. Perhaps, I thought, this was normal behaviour before shrugging and returning the bucket to its rightful place.

As I approached Rose Cottage I thought it looked a bit forlorn and somewhat worse for wear. I accepted this due to what had happened but what I did get cross at, was the sight of the damage to the borders. Almost every area had been flattened and the beautiful plants had mostly been trodden flat.

I let myself in and wandered about, almost in a daze. The only place I was unable to access was the larder, which was sealed by a sticker and warned of dire consequences should anybody enter. There was no way I could replenish my now empty sugar bowl or retrieve anything else I might desire in the way of snacks. I quietly laughed to myself as I swiftly realised I had no sugar left anyhow. In resignation, I looked at my watch and decided to go to the pub. It was only now, that I realised I was still wearing the same eclectic mix of clothes I had on from the day before. Even so, I felt half-presentable, so left the cottage, and walked to the car. I stopped, turned and looked at the view and then looked up at the skies before shrugging. Following this little ritual I decided to walk to the pub, since I realised I might exceed my usual consumption of alcohol. I felt very low. I couldn't understand how things were not as they should be in my life. This was supposed to have been my little haven away from the chaos of life's trials and tribulations.

All I wanted now was for the quiet way of life I had hoped for to finally begin.

The Silver Plough was fairly empty, since I arrived there so early. Stephen greeted me and commented on both my clothing and the earlier police activity. His choice and order of wording, made me feel self-conscious since he mentioned my clothing well before the 'goings on' at Rose Cottage. Unaware of this, he poured me a glass of white wine before stoking the fire. Here though, I felt comfortable, but was nagged by a feeling that I should be doing something. After my first glass of wine, I remembered two very important syllables. 'PAR-TAY!' It screamed at me as I sunk my head into my hands. What would Joel think of me now? Being without a phone, meant I had no way of getting hold of him. Of course, I could have used the pubs landline but I only knew Joel's number as speed dial number one. Technology had made me lazy and remembering door entry numbers, bank details, pin numbers and passwords had all but clogged up my brain. As far as phone numbers were concerned, I could barely remember my own. This experience just made me want to forget everything else life had to offer. I just needed another drink, so I ordered a bottle.

It wasn't long before some of the locals began to appear and for once, I was greeted more cordially. There were even drinks 'sent my way' by some well-wishers, which was a welcome reminder of what I had only recently expected from living in an area like this.

There was light banter but no mention of what had happened at Rose Cottage. For once, I felt the need to talk to others about the subject but it just wasn't happening. However, by the time I left I didn't seem to mind, because I had achieved two things. Firstly, I felt like I belonged and secondly, I felt rather tipsy.

As I walked, or should I more accurately say, lurched down the lane, I thought about my so-called trials and tribulations. Once again, I thought of all the grief I had recently endured. Strangely, I knew I had the means to leave all this behind me and disappear forever. But somehow, this didn't seem like an option, partly due to what had just taken place in the pub.

I must have looked a curious sight as I teetered down the lane and back towards the cottage. From behind, I heard my name being called, "Claire…, Claire… Stop!"

I almost fell over as I turned to face the person calling me, "Oh, Robin. I've just been to the pub." Why I felt the need to tell him where I had been was beyond me. Apart from that, I think it was obvious.

Robin wobbled as his bike came to a sudden halt, "I've just had word from the police…, to say that they have been trying…, to get hold of you… They want to speak with you… Something…, to do with Julianne…, I think." He gasped breathlessly. His sweaty brow and shaky voice confirmed the strenuous efforts he had put into find me. Robin took off his cap and used it to wipe his brow. He replaced the hat upon his grey hair, which had darkened with sweat and was sitting lank on his head.

I approached him and tried to keep my balance as I did, "I hope it is something to do with Julianne, otherwise I'm in trouble." I couldn't help but giggle as the last few words left my lips.

Robin looked at me in disappointment, and I can understand why. Without another word, he lifted his bike and turned it around as if in disgust, as I called out after him, "Robin…, Robin…, Please? I'm sorry! It's just that things are a bit…" My want was to cry but I couldn't. After all, what did I have to cry about? The man before me had sustained more misery than I could ever comprehend, despite the losses in my life. "Robin!" I shouted once more. "I meant what I said about being sorry. I am sure you've had times when you didn't know what to do next. Well, I'm at that stage now. What happens next? What should I be doing now?"

Knowing Robin had a problem with his hearing made me realise that I might have just wasted my breath. Surprisingly, Robin stopped in his tracks, turned, and looked at me sympathetically. No longer breathless he said, "I do know how you feel. We are all going through a bad time at the moment. For some it is worse than for others. By the way, the police have confirmed Julianne's identity and cause of death. They have also told me that I can arrange her funeral. I want you to sit with Liz and me on the day. Tuesday week, at eleven."

Once again, I hated myself. I gratefully agreed and watched him ride away. I had, by now, more than sobered up, certainly enough to make me realise what a fool I had just been. I cursed myself before walking home in a much more sedate manner. Then a part of his sentence struck me... and struck me hard! The words 'cause of death' had a profound effect on me as I recalled the damage I had noticed on Julianne's neck. I paused for a moment or two before gathering my thoughts back to that day.

It wasn't long before I heard another sound from behind me. A car drew up alongside, "Hello Miss Chambers. Can I give you a lift home?"

There was no mistaking the soothing voice of DI Hockley.

Chapter 27

In The Wake Of Time

I made coffee but could not bear to drink it without sugar; however, DI Hockley seemed to enjoy it. No matter how drunk I was or how sobering black, sugarless coffee could be, I could, and would, never drink it.

The policeman took his time and, for a while, watched me from over the rim of his mug before speaking, "We are making progress in our enquiries and have a few questions for you. Elimination and all that sort of thing. I think you have to understand why we are asking, don't you?"

Somehow, the question seemed odd, but since I had never been in this sort of situation before I was quite happy to help, "Of course."

His lines of enquires were unusual to say the least and I could see no connection to it at all, "Now, can you tell me how you came to buy this place?" He gestured with his free hand as if to encompass the room.

I, in turn looked around me and smiled, "Well..." I faltered slightly since I too had asked myself the self-same question, "...I saw it online and thought it would be nice to move away from the city. You see, there was an auction and I happened to be the lucky winner."

DI Hockley placed his empty mug down, "Now, here you see I am confused, because I have spoken to a Mr Glasspool about the sale and he had raised some questions." I looked both quizzical and astounded by the fact that Mr Glasspool was now involved, "He tells me that you were rather eager to purchase this property and I want to know why."

Would he believe me if I told him about the nightmare I had endured, which eventually brought me here in the first place? I wasn't sure he was the right sort of man who would understand computers so I kept my answer simple, "Look around you. It is perfect and who wouldn't like to live here?" Although with hindsight, even I would have second thoughts.

He leant forward and rested his right arm on his knee, "Yes, I can see that but what I want to know, is how it is that you got to know about the place? Mr

Glasspool was cynical in his answer and told me that you were informed of the sale by a friend of yours. Is this true?"

For some reason I felt like I was being accused of something so I decided to tell him the truth, "Well it wasn't as simple as that you see. My computer found it for me. Um, I mean, I turned on my computer one day and there it was. Well, it wasn't obvious what I was looking at first but..." I stopped talking since even I had difficulty in understanding what I was trying to say.

DI Hockley looked at me curiously, "BUT! But what? No, don't continue... I believe you, although the evidence from our lab boys say that they can find no trace about the site on your computer any earlier than when it was on general release. Not that that is really important at the moment. As you know, I am still trying to solve a cold case, which by the way, I know you had no involvement in."

In some respects I found the latter part of his sentence quite a relief, but then put me on the defensive "So why the questions? I mean, why is it important for you to know how I came to own this place? As if I haven't been through enough already..." The last few words were almost a whisper as I trailed off the sentence.

He stood up, "Of course you are right. It is that, so much had already eluded me when this first started, that I didn't want anything to be left out this time. Anyhow, thanks for the coffee. I'll bid you farewell."

By the time we reached the front door, I felt relieved he was going and even started to question my role in all of this.

He turned just as I was about to close the door, "Oh, by the way. What do you know about your family's connection to this area?"

I was stunned and it took me several moments to answer, "My family?" I queried, "None." I thought hard before adding, "None to my knowledge."

Without saying another word, he nodded, smiled, and then walked to his car.

I watched as he reversed from his parked position and drove away leaving me feeling tired and confused.

As soon as his car was out of sight, I left through the back door to seek out Crinchley. I found him in a meadow about a mile from the cottage. I called out and watched as his sheep scattered from around him, "Crinchley."

With his head held low, he walked towards me, "Hi Claire, is everything okay?"

I nodded before placing my hand under his chin and lifting it so I could look him in the eye, "What do you know about my family?"

There was no hint of a lie, "Your family? Nothing. Why?"

With my hand still on his chin I asked again, "Did, or do you know anybody in my family?"

Once again, his answer convinced me I was being told the truth, "Look Claire, I didn't know your family and would have told you long ago if I had. Can you please tell me why you are asking?"

I stepped back and felt somewhat deflated, "Oh, I don't know. It is just something that policeman asked me as he left a moment a go."

Crinchley offered his hand and led me to a fallen tree, which made a convenient bench, "Soup?" It was not what I expected to be offered but it was received with a welcome smile. The wind was harsh and cold at the top end of the meadow where I first spoke to Crinchley. Here it was much calmer and warmer. He asked me what I had been quizzed about so I told him, "Strange. Perhaps he has a special method in interrogation techniques. I know when I was interviewed by him in the past he asked me what my favourite colour was. Never understood the question then and still don't to this day. You know what... I bet you he just said that to see how you would react.

Nah, I wouldn't worry about it. He is a good policeman but this case is his last and one he wants to tie up. Don't worry; I'm sure it's nothing."

During the period of time leading up to Julianne's funeral, I experienced a plethora of emotions and experiences. Mostly, they centred on what had happened in the cottage during the day and occasionally at night. Thereafter, a series of other strange events occurred. Predominantly, these occurrences were confined to sounds, although there were a few occasions when I saw things from the corner of my eye. Mostly, the sounds consisted of scrapes, bangs and footsteps. What I found most disturbing though, were the voices. They were so intense I could still hear them even when I covered my ears. It was then, that I decided it was my imagination and from then on, chose to ignore them. Although that, was easier said than done!

The closer the funeral came though - the louder the sounds became. On one occasion, I was woken by the sound of chanting:

Cry for the little girl who lived in the ground
Cry for the little girl who has now been found
Cry for the little girl who lives all alone
Cry for the little girl who was trapped by the stone
Cry for the little girl who lost all her kin
Cry for the little girl who hides from her sin.

No matter how hard I tried, I could not get the verse out of my head. I even tried to hum another tune to drown it out, but even this would eventually incorporate the words.

For some reason, the night before the funeral, everything went silent, but a single event occurred… something quite significant.

At some time during the night, I awoke feeling ill at ease about something and went to the kitchen on a hunch. Here I looked around, and for some reason checked to see if the larder was still sealed off, which it was. I then noticed a light coming from within the gaps around the door. Slowly, I peeled back the police tape and opened it - not quite knowing what to expect. I froze, since before me stood Julianne. She was glowing from head to foot in green luminosity… everything about her was so alive. She looked so different from the little girl I had seen in all our previous encounters. She whispered sweetly, "Can I come in?" I smiled and was about to let her in when I remembered all of the warnings I had received throughout, *'You mustn't invite her in!'* Suddenly, these five short words struck fear into my heart. I tried to calm myself and silently questioned the thought… Surely, they didn't mean her. It was a difficult choice but I quietly said 'no'. I held my breath and waited for the wrath of hell to be unleashed before me. Instead, she simply smiled back before seamlessly moving downwards and fading away into the ether.

Although I couldn't sleep after that, the rest of the night remained calm and the morning brought rays of sunshine into the room. The day was to remain bright but cold. Dressed with the colder weather in mind, I walked to the Alsford's where I was greeted by Robin. We spoke briefly of the weather before he took me into the familiar surroundings of their kitchen. Liz took me by the hand and guided me to a seat where I was made comfortable. Outwardly, she appeared calm although I sensed a certain amount of anxiety in her voice, "It won't be long now. Tea?"

I declined and due to my nervousness asked if I could use the toilet. I was shown a door at the end of a corridor. When I entered, I was amazed at the simplicity of it. 'Functional' was the best way I could describe it and 'tiny' certainly illustrated its dimensions but there was something there I had certainly not expected. On the back of the door was a pentagram scratched deep into the woodwork. The sight of this caused me a certain amount of concern and I wondered why it was there at all. The pentagram, I was sure, had always been associated with witchcraft and I assumed that the symbol before me was proof that either Liz or Robin had a connection. I was confused and questioned why would either of Julianne's parents be involved in witchcraft? Did they know more about Julianne's disappearance than they were letting on? If so, how could they react to what had recently happened in the manner they were doing now? All of these questions needed answering and I was now beginning to doubt who knew what... and who I could trust.

I returned to the kitchen and found it crowded with people, and believe me a crowd in such a small kitchen was not difficult to achieve. One person caught my eye and assumed it was the undertaker. He was talking to Robin when I entered the room and stopped talking when he noticed me. His smile exposed crooked yellowing teeth, which gave me the creeps. A shallow nod of his head added to this feeling of unease. It was not long before he approached me and introduced himself, "Bernard Royston Adams at your service. I understand you are now living in the cottage. Rose Cottage, that is." I merely nodded as I watched his lips move whilst still maintaining the glimmer of a smile. He added, "I buried Miss Adams... no relation. God rest her tormented soul."

With that, he walked away and shook hands with another unknown mourner. Why had he added the bit about her 'tormented soul' I wondered? My brow furrowed but not for long as Liz approached me once more, "Thank you, Claire. Thank you for being here.

You are to come with me in the car. It is not far and it is important that you be there with us since I know Julianne would have wanted it that way."

Before I could ask questions, Robin called out asking for everybody's attention, "The cars are here so I suggest we leave. I shall be walking ahead of the car and... and..." He could not continue as his eyes welled up and his voice broke. Liz went to his side to offer him comfort as he turned to leave. They left together, and I followed closely, the last to leave the kitchen.

The brightness outside was almost blinding, and most peculiar for this time of morning and year. There was a touch of spring in the air despite it still being several months off.

The church was packed and I was convinced the whole village had turned out to bid Julianne farewell. However, no matter how hard I looked, I could not see Crinchley, although I did see Bill who grimly sat alone. It was as if he sensed my gaze and looked up. He nodded my way and gave me an uneasy soulful look. One other person stood out from the crowd, and this time it was not me. D I Hockley stood alone and to one side of the church but close enough to observe the faces of those around me. I just knew he would make a beeline for me at the end of the service.

Julianne was finally laid to rest next to her grandmother, just as I was sure I would one day be next to mine. I didn't know whether this was a comforting thought, but it was certainly a sobering one.

At the end of the service, I looked at the flowers and felt a huge twinge of guilt when I realised I had not contributed in any way towards this mark of respect. I vowed to make good by swearing to pay regular visits instead. I did, however, find a small posy amongst some of the vast wreaths. The posy stood out, mainly due to its simplicity and the beautiful colours of the late winter pansies. There was no evidence of who had left them, but I knew it was Crinchley.

From the church, there was to be a gathering at the Silver Plough, but for some reason there were very few people there. In fact, apart from Liz and DI Hockley the only other people to attend were a small group of local drinkers. Even Robin had chosen to keep away from the rest of the people, instead choosing the company of his closest friends, leaving Liz to stand alone. DI Hockley and I approached her at the same time and both spoke at once. DI Hockley apologised and allowed me to speak first, "Mrs Alsford... Liz. Thank you for inviting me here today. I feel honoured and in a way, humbled by the experience. Julianne is at peace now. And now you can go and see her from time to time."

I had not prepared my little dialogue but I felt I needed to say something and it needed to be personal to her. She smiled and thanked me for my kind words. The only words she added, were to inform me that from then on, she would visit Julianne's grave every day. DI Hockley was about to continue what he had started to say when Liz nodded to us both and left. It was soon after she left that Robin got up and followed.

The mood in the bar was understandably sombre and it remained silent for quite a while before I grabbed DI Hockley's arm. I led him to a far corner, "Why would somebody have a pentagram sign in their house?"

He looked at me curiously, "Why would whom?" I declined to say but I'm convinced he knew. He continued, "Oh! Well, the pentagram is not what most people think it is. You see, the pentagram represents the number 5 and is usually there to ward off evil. In mythology, the number 5 is important in many ways. For instance, we commonly have five toes on each foot. Likewise, there are five fingers on each hand. There are also five senses as well as five stages of life..."

I interrupted him since I understood the point and felt somewhat relieved that I had mistakenly believed that the sign was for evil purposes only. His knowledge of the subject made me ask, "How come you know so much about the subject? I thought you would just humour me and say something about witches or something."

He let out a hollow laugh, "Humour you? Now why would I want to do that? No, I'm afraid it comes with the turf. Being in this neck of the woods means you have to know a little about a lot… especially folklore."

I wanted to know more about Rose Cottage's background, but he excused himself before I could ask, "Sorry, can't chat right now. Oh, before I go. I shall have some answers for you by late today, since the lab boys are finalising their results as we speak."

With that, he left, leaving me feeling very vulnerable and alone despite there being a few friendly faces about. It was all rather strange really; here I was among the very people who had at one time seen me as an outsider. Remarkably, in a relatively short space of time, I had gone from an outsider to an excepted member of their community.

I too decided I would leave and slowly headed for home.

Chapter 28

A Time Of Reckoning

As I approached my home, I felt a chill and sensed that something was wrong. The basis of this feeling was purely to do with sound, as I heard an unusual noise coming from within the cottage. The sound was mechanical and something I had heard before but never experienced first-hand. I approached the front door and after noticing that the door was slightly ajar, I entered with caution.

I called out several times but there was no answer, just the incessant machine-driven sound coming from the back of the building. From the safety of the front door, I peeked in and saw something that caused me to run into the room.

When I reached Crinchley, I thought he was dead as he was slumped over the arm of my sofa. A trickle of blood was coming from a small cut in a very large bruised area on his forehead. He must have been there for some time, since a pool of blood had seeped into the fabric of the cushion from where his head had lain. I thought this rather odd, since the cushion was out of place and appeared to have been placed there deliberately. Strangely, it had been placed as if to make him more comfortable. Outlandish as that seems, none of what I could see or hear made any sense.

Shaking, I approached the kitchen door quietly, although if I had made a noise it would not have been heard above the racket coming from within. What I saw alarmed me, although what I then heard above the machine-driven sound was just as distressing.

There, with his back to me was Bill, still dressed in his Sunday best. He appeared to be attacking the hinges of the back door with an angle grinder. Sparks were flying in all directions, giving the whole spectacle a bizarre framework. His determination was obvious and some of what he was saying sounded foreign to my ears, "The women of Satan hear me now. I cast thee from out and I will pay my part in Hell along with you all. De la iad și la eternitate am aruncat spiritele voastre josnice dincolo de mormânt de stăpânul tău! Hear me! Hear me! I shall no longer live this lie..."

It was as if he sensed my presence as he suddenly stopped and turned around to face me. His face was distorted and drenched in sweat. In places, there were dotted dark pits where the sparks from the angle iron had hit his unprotected face, "Fereste-te de abordările Witch și ea poartă voință bolnavă și moartea celor care îndrăznesc să intre în felul ei! Do not stop me..." With that, he turned and continued in his task with absolute determination and sheer bloody mindedness.

I didn't know what to do. I stood rooted to the spot but was soon distracted by a loud groan from behind me. I spun around to see Crinchley trying to get to his feet, but he failed in doing so and once more collapsed. As I approached him, my attention was diverted by another distraction, this time coming from the front door, "Cooey! Is there anybody there? It is me, Ida... Ida Evans... Bill's wife. Is he in there?"

I felt a wave of relief and started to walk towards the door, but was soon stopped short by a sharp pain that started at the back of my head before shooting to the frontal lobe. I screamed at what seemed like a thousand voices entering my head at the same time. The pressure was such that it caused me to buckle under the strain. My hand immediately reached for my head as I screamed out, "Ida, please help me! Please, please come and help me. He is attacking me!

Help!" As the last syllable left my lips, the pain disappeared and the only thing to replace it was the continuing sound of the angle grinder in the near distance. I looked behind and could see nothing apart from the unconscious form of Crinchley on the floor. Bill was nowhere to be seen, although I could still hear him cursing in a foreign voice.

The front door slammed shut with a tremendous bang and Ida entered the room.

It was only now that I realised I had neither seen nor met her at any point since my arrival. She looked down at me and smiled, showing a row of rotten teeth. It was as if she was gliding across the floor and as she passed I felt an icy cold blast of air, which seemed to pierce my heart. No matter what I did, I could not move. In fact, the more I tried the more the carpet beneath appeared to want to consume me. I was soon pulled to the ground by an invisible but powerful force.

It wasn't long before I heard a scream. It was the scream of a man in extreme pain before utter silence. No longer was there the sound of machine, or of a man's voice as they both fell silent simultaneously.

Still caught in my struggle to get to my feet I looked towards the kitchen door as the menacing figure of Ida returned. Her cupped hands were blood red and in the centre was a slow beating heart. I wanted to scream but even this was impossible, as my eyes were fixated on her as she approached me. She laughed, "Thank you Claire. Thank you for inviting me in. I wasn't sure it was going to be as easy as that but you see I needed your permission before I could enter. I'm sorry about Bill, but he can be such a fusspot, you know. He has no heart for what I do best." As she cackled she looked around the room, "My… you have done wonders my dear. Mabel would be pleased to see it like this, and even more pleased to see the threshold back to where it rightfully belongs. Oh, how they thought they had us beaten but they did not reckon on you coming along… although I knew this day would come!" She crowed.

My head now felt like it was getting heavier and I was having extreme trouble trying to keep it off the ground. Somehow, I knew if my head hit the carpet then I was finished.

Ida circled me, "What's wrong my treasure? Cat got your tongue? Oh! Of course, you cannot speak, can you?" She snapped her fingers, and I swear I saw blue sparks fly from them as she did so.

As an instantaneous response to her rhetoric I found my voice, "You evil bitch! What have you done?"

Although I could now speak, I could barely move my diaphragm. She now stood before me, "Now, now my girl, that is no way for a lady like you to behave." She mocked before adding, "No, of all people I expected more from you."

I didn't know what to make of her words as they implied we had a connection, "What..., do you..., mean..., by that?" I asked breathlessly. My chest now hurt as I spoke. Each word felt like it was draining my life away.

She laughed again and started circling me once more, "You have no idea at all, have you?" I wanted to ask the obvious but no longer had the strength, "Now Claire, there must be somebody you know who we are connected to. Do you have a particular name in mind?"

My brain ached and the voices that had previously warned me about letting her in were now trying to creep back into my head. Each and every one of what seemed like a hundred voices needed a separate platform to speak from. As hard as I tried, I did not have the capacity to listen to any of them as I continued to struggle, "What are..., you talking..., about..., you mad bitch?" I thought harder and harder. The only name I could muster was the only one I had not before encountered until I came here, "Are you..., talking..., about..., Marcie..., because I don't..."

She cackled louder than before and repeated the name sarcastically before I could finish speaking, "Marcie! Ha, ha, ha…! Oh, my dear child… How wrong you are. Oh, I'm going to enjoy this! Marcie isn't one person. No, not one… but three! You see…, I was brought up in an orphanage with two like-minded friends. This was many years ago and we lived together in a rather grand old house. You may have heard of it… *Ridgeway House!!*" She taunted, *"Ring any bells?"*

I was so shocked at hearing the name Ridgeway House that I could no longer support my head. Reluctantly, I succumbed to the pressure by lying down completely. Ida got to her knees and taunted me further, "Ah! You didn't know, did you? You coming here had nothing to do with…" She laughed once more breathing out a foul odour, "Oh, how absolutely delicious. You see Claire… the name Marcie was made up from three names… Mabel Adams, Rose Chambers and Ida Evans!"

The middle name hit me like a sledgehammer and I screamed…! There was now strength in my voice and I lifted my head, "Nanny Rose wouldn't have had anything to do with the likes of you. She married and…"

My sentence was cut short, "She never married that idiot! He was just a means to an end and I made sure he didn't stay around for long. Anyways, your ever-loving Nanny Rose's so-called husband provided us with the means to fund this property. It was one of the many we had in our portfolio."

With sheer determination, I managed to get to my knees, which seemed to surprise Ida, "My…, you are a fighter. I'll give you that. Perhaps some of your Nan still lives in you, although, even she succumbed to me in the end. She betrayed us you know. When Julianne found out what we were up to, I had to do something about it. Your poor old Nan had a very simplistic outlook on life and thought that our…" She paused slightly and seemed to take relish in my discomfort, "… our talents should be used for the good. I, on the other hand, saw this as a weakness on her part. The rift caused her to leave us to carry on our own. Of course, without her, we were much weaker and had to make do, but as soon as you came on the scene…" She paused in delight, "…I, as the only survivor, suddenly became stronger. My, I've counted these days for my powers to increase!"

She dropped the now motionless heart by her side, "W-w-what about Bill?" I stammered.

She lifted her foot and was about to stamp on it, "Bill?! Bill knew something was amiss but didn't know what. Huh, I even convinced him that Crinchley had something to do with Julianne's disappearance and with a little bit of encouragement, he took it upon himself to… Now what was it he said? Oh, yes, 'sort it out.'" She sniggered before frowning, "And what a mess he made of that. No, it was only after the door was put back in place and my powers really started to return that he fully understood. He had no choice but to trap you in the cellar… I forced him too. Although he couldn't even do that right could he? He was typically weak and afraid."

The more she spoke the more my strength returned. When it did, I managed to lash out, throwing her off balance. I knew the heart was of some importance to her and managed to knock it under the settee, and out of reach. From where she lay, she cursed, "Lucifer, îți poruncesc cu loialitatea mea o formă de respect din acest actuală!"

Immediately, my body rose off the ground by about half a metre or so. Involuntarily, my arms stretched outwards and my legs pulled apart causing me to look like a star… A Pentagram! It was only then, that I thought of DI Hockley and his interpretation of the pentagram. For some reason this caused me to laugh. My laughter caught Ida by surprise and a fleeting look of confusion crossed her face. I didn't know or understand the words that came from my lips, "Din moartea celor de ori plecat de, ei, înainte de a începe să mă urc!" With that, she rolled from where she lay and to my utmost amazement continued to roll up the wall and onto the ceiling. With her concentration diverted, I fell to the ground. Ida cursed and swore in at least four languages that, for some reason, I now understood.

There was more commotion as Ida started to mumble before roaring out a single sentence, "Descărcarea de gestiune!" With that, she fell to the floor, got up, ran into the kitchen as quickly as she could.

With remarkable agility and pace, I found myself almost next to her and struck her hard, which knocked her to the floor. Although standing over her, I held the upper hand for a very short while, since I stepped back and tripped over the outstretched body of Bill. I was left winded and scrabbled to get up but couldn't, as I felt myself slip and slide on Bill's spilt blood. I looked across… his face was as white as snow on a first laying.

Ida took advantage of my situation and gathered her wits, "As strong as you are getting, I have more experience than you and shall send you to perdition…" She raised her hand and started to mumble. In doing so, I felt an invisible icy hand at my throat. With every gulping breath I made, the grip tightened until I almost blacked out under the pressure. Trying as hard as I could, I could no longer defend myself and started to relax. This period of enforced relaxation was a turning point in my understanding, as what appeared before me in the darkness was none other than my Father, "Dad!" I screamed. At first, I merely noticed his youthful face and the tighter the grip around my neck the more I saw of him. He was wearing a black suit that had white chalk-like symbols upon it - but the symbols were animated. Each symbol appeared to move around his clothing in fluid motions, and now and again one or more of the symbols would glow brightly.

He smiled and spoke softly, "Hello Kookie. I should have missed you but I haven't since I have been and still am part of your life, even now. Before you go, I want you to know how much I love you. Although I didn't want you to endure so much pain, it was a necessary evil so you could understand." He handed me something before continuing, "As a Warlock, I knew much of what would happen here today. I am here to help you through it. Goodbye, my beautiful daughter, don't be afraid."

His vision faded and I could once more hear Ida cackling as she started to rant louder. My eyes opened and the blackness faded as I concentrated all my efforts on one thing. Ida realised something was about to happen but didn't know what. Far too late, she looked to her left before being violently knocked off her feet by a flying tackle. Together they hit the ground, but Crinchley could do no more as he was far too weak due to the original blow to the head he had received from Bill. Ida knew she had to turn her immediate attentions away from me. Instantly, she turned her full concentration and efforts toward Crinchley. What she was doing to him was plain to see as he suddenly began to waver before beating at his clothes with his hands. It was as if he was reliving the past and appeared to be engulfed in invisible flames. Smoke without flames started to pour from his clothes as he screamed and writhed before collapsing to the floor in a quivering heap.

Somehow, though, I did not feel as useless as I had before and was about to add to the melee, "Ida listen to me and listen good..." As I spoke, my bracelet glowed brightly and became extremely hot without burning. I then noticed a whitish blue glow coming from around the frame of the back door and a familiar voice boomed out from the other side, "Stai în spate copilul meu!" A second, more diminutive voice then called out, "Claire! Where in God's name are you? What is going on in there and what the hell is all that noise?" The noise Joel was referring to was that of Ida shrieking in response to hearing the first voice... that of Nanny Rose's!

Ida faced the back door as her shrieking got louder and more insistent before the most remarkable sight I have ever seen caught me by surprise. In either frustration or determination to gain my attention, Joel hammered on the back door.

Whichever, the consequences were about to reverberate throughout the entire county.

The door, already weakened by Bill's handiwork, collapsed inwardly and fell on top of Ida. Her screams could both be heard and seen, as a shockwave of redness appeared to emanate from the core of the scene. Above this, there was the very pronounced sound of cracking, as bone was crushed to a pulp under the full mass of the heavy door.

Joel was oblivious to what had just happened and unceremoniously stepped in through the doorway. He stood atop the door whilst surveying the grisly scene before him. It must have looked a ghastly sight as I stood in between the unconscious body of one man and the bloody corpse of another. Knowing Joel, he was about to say something quite astounding, but what happened next caught his and my attention. There was a slight rumbling from beneath Joel's feet. Without warning, the door inextricably began to disintegrate under his weight.

With lightning speed, Joel backtracked and looked on in astonishment as the door dissolved into a pile of dust. A sudden wind came in, scooped up the dust before filtering through the fine powder. The dust whirled around the room gently before exiting through the opening and into the garden. I watched in amazement as the ground-up remains of both the door and Ida then separated into several individual clouds. There was a rumble of thunder, as each cloud appeared to simultaneously fly in different directions before disappearing from sight.

On the floor and ahead of Joel's feet were just a few metal studs, a door handle and the twisted remnants of a few rusty screws. Apart from this, the only discernible evidence of the doors existence, were three badly damaged hinges.

Joel looked up sheepishly and said in a hushed voice, "Sorry!"

What I heard next was, I am convinced, only heard by me, "Prezența răul produce acum la un loc de iad și de ședere fi plecat pentru totdeauna!" Once again, it was the unmistakable voice of Nanny Rose.

I looked at Joel and smiled seconds before I felt a warm glow in my hand. I looked down and opened my hand to see what my Father had given me. It was this that appeared to give me the strength to pull myself out of the darkness earlier…

…it was his wedding ring!

Chapter 29

Restitution Before Restoration

I now live in more settled and tranquil surroundings with my cat Priscilla Jane. Priscilla Jane is a very petite black cat who turned up on my doorstep the day after Ida disappeared.

Much more happened after that particular day, but none more so than the realisation of my new found powers. Dad's wedding band now hangs from a long silver chain and sits snuggly between my cleavage. I feel stronger having it lay so close to my heart and knowing I never did lose either my parents or Nanny Rose... This helped me cope with what happened immensely.

To get to this point in my life, I had to endure more than one person should have had to cope with. On reflection, it was a journey well worth living. To get to where I am now and on the way, I learnt many new things. None more so, than details about my mystical heritage. Yes, I am now truly happy in the knowledge of my true identity.

I did however, see my family once more and with that vision came a further and welcomed explanation.

Nanny Rose was the matriarch of the coven and only ever wanted to use her powers for the good. However, Mabel's reluctance to accept her own powers meant that Ida could easily prey upon her indecisiveness. With two powers against her, Nanny Rose eventually left the coven, especially since she had just become a grandmother. There was though, apparently, a much more sinister reason behind the breakup of the coven. Although Nanny Rose knew of Ida's appetite for more power, she was unaware of how desperate she was to gain it. To achieve this goal, Ida felt the need to offer sacrifices. Goats and sheep were no longer enough to satisfy her needs, so she proposed to Mabel a human sacrifice. Although Mabel thought this was a step too far, she complied. This also explained something Bill once said when he innocently referred to cot deaths… fortunately; Bill never did know the truth behind those deaths.

As Ida's powers increased, Nanny Rose decided that there was only one way to weaken her. By leaving, she curtailed Ida's ability to become too strong, although she still remained a force to be reckoned with. Over the ensuing years, Ida did what she could to try to retain what she had. Julianne was her swansong, which kept her going until I arrived on the scene. She knew if she could take me, then she would regain everything and more!

Meanwhile, Nanny Rose knew her own powers would be transferred to her kin in some form or other. True to form, her son… my Father, eventually developed more powers than she could have ever imagined. Due to his loving upbringing, the powers he possessed were only used on very rare occasions, and even then, only if he felt they were absolutely necessary. This meant, that on 9/11 when he realised his beloved wife was about to be taken from him, he had to make a choice. In the early stages of the disaster, he had sensed something was about to happen and used his craft to transfer himself across to be by her side. Here, he was only able to protect her to the point of slowing down the process and only then, just enough for her to get out of the building. What happened after that was telling about the man… and the Warlock. With the knowledge of her impending death, he decided that he did not want to live without her and chose to stay with his cherished wife. Between them, they were to spend eternity in a realm that was neither in this world nor in the next. This was the price he had to pay for making the choices he did.

On the other hand, Nanny Rose had vowed to keep quiet about what she really knew about my Father and the ties she had with her own background. There was a point following the subsequent disappearance of my Father, that she thought about telling me but she didn't. Somehow, I think she regretted that decision and wished to, somehow, make amends… that, she eventually did.

When Nanny Rose died, she tried to tell me about the cottage and her last words reflected this, but I misheard. The word 'Mercy' was in fact 'Marcie'! I also learned that Ida struck when Nan was least expecting it. By casting a certain spell against Nanny Rose, Ida had inadvertently set in motion other events that would also seal her own fate.

Both my parents and Nanny Rose were bound by certain constraints over my life. Between them, they explained that they wanted to intervene on several occasions but couldn't. No matter how hard they tried, they failed and eventually had to resort to some pretty desperate measures to gain my attention. For some, they apologised.

As for Joel, he told me that he had a phone call from me, begging for both forgiveness for missing the party and help. This happened on the morning of his unintentional intervention, and well in advance of Ida's involvement. He clearly stated that it was me who rang him, although he also admitted that the conversation did seem out of character. He almost decided not to come but felt a strange compulsion to do so. I know I didn't make the call and have a fair idea how it came about, although I'm not complaining. Since our reunion, Joel and I have become closer, almost to the point of him spending more time with me now than at any other time in the past. He has become accustomed to the occasional strange goings on in the cottage, and either turns a blind eye to them or knows more than he lets on. He even accepts my legacy of being a white witch, and although still not keen on sheep, understands the message they tried to convey the day they inadvertently frightened him, and the night they approached me in the fields. They were, in their way trying to communicate their awareness of my presence, and their relief that I had finally arrived to free them from the horror of Ida's cruel sacrifices.

The underground chamber at Rose Cottage has been fully secured and converted into a cosy study for myself. Joel knows better than to venture down there, and confessed to me that that was the one place in the house that still gives him the 'Willies'.

It wasn't long before the back door was replaced by a beautiful light oak stable door. Both Martyn and Noah produced some of their best work in creating the replacement, although both were surprised by my insistence of having a pentagram carved into it.

Remarkably, the doll's house mirrored this change well before it happened, which made me realise that the smaller version of the real thing reflected the future. Somehow, they are both linked and the doll's house acts as a magical barometer, which in turn now helps me keep one-step ahead.

Likewise, the stream now has a purpose made arched oak bridge, complete with handrails. The bench still stands and is one of my most favourite spots in the garden. Often I just sit there and admire the all-round views whilst deep in thought.

As far as the police were concerned, DI Hockley concluded that Ida was the driving force behind the death of Julianne, with the possibility of at least two accomplices. From the photograph, they could only positively identify Bill, Ida and Mabel. He also concluded that Ida had killed her own husband after he had confessed of his wife's part in Julianne's disappearance. He did this by leaving a message on the police stations answering service. The police believed it to be Bill's voice, and also believed that when Ida found out, she killed him before escaping into hiding. They were convinced she, or at least her body, would turn up one day. Nobody seemed that bothered about spending too much time in searching for her.

DI Hockley did however, have one puzzle he could not explain. He confided in me by asking if my grandmother had ever touched the peg that was found hanging in the window. The reason he gave was that it was her fingerprints found upon it. He compared it to one that was filed with the MoD where she worked on a secret project during the war. I, of course, said it was quite possible that it was one of hers, which I might have packed when I left home. He accepted this and never mentioned it again… even though, in truth, the pegs were recently bought new. Nor did he mention the connection to the area and Nanny Rose. Perhaps these points were no longer important to him, or he was just glad to be retiring after solving a case that had haunted him since his career in C.I.D. had started.

Finally, Crinchley made a remarkable recovery due to a 'strange' and medically unknown phenomenon. This so-called 'miracle' caused his dermis, epidermis and subcutaneous tissue to heal. Over a period of a year, his disfigurement and muscle damage started to reverse, meaning that his looks and physical abilities returned. Remarkably, even his eyesight reverted to full working order. Some say, this was due to the ordeal he had endured on the day of Bill's death and Ida's disappearance… others, were not so sure. I, on the other hand, knew otherwise.

Our friendship blossomed and we became very, very close as the years went by.

On my part, I funded the rebuild of his house and insisted that he had proper plumbing installed…

…There was no way I was ever going to pee in a bucket again!

The following is a translation from English to Romanian:

"From hell and to eternity I cast your vile spirits beyond the grave of your master!" - "De la iad și la eternitate am aruncat spiritele voastre josnice dincolo de mormânt de stăpânul tău!"

"Beware the witch approaches and she bears ill will and death to those who dare get in her way!" - "Fereste-te de abordările Witch și ea poartă voință bolnavă și moartea celor care îndrăznesc să intre în felul ei!"

"Lucifer, I command you with my allegiance, some form of respect from this cur!" - "Lucifer, îți poruncesc cu loialitatea mea o formă de respect din acest actuală!"

“From the death of those of times gone by, make her before me start to climb” - “Din moartea celor de ori plecat de, ei, înainte de a începe să mă urc!"

"Stand back my child!" - "Stai în spate copilul meu!"

“Evil presence now yield to a place of hell and stay be gone forever!” -“Prezența răul produce acum la un loc de iad și de ședere fi plecat pentru totdeauna!”

If you have a few spare minutes, please visit Amazon.com & Amazon.co.uk and write a review for my book. Your objective review will help other potential readers make informed choices.

Many thanks

Shelby Locke

Language: UK English Spellings